I Will Always Love You

MAGIC PROSE Publishing
publisher@magicprose.com

ISBN: 1-4936-5783-6
ISBN-13: 9781493657834
Library of Congress Control Number: 2013920878
CreateSpace Independent Publishing Platform, North Charleston, SC

I Will Always Love You

Belinda Vasquez Garcia

Dedication

This book is dedicated to the victims of 9/11.

And if this shall be my last breath,
I will love you even more after death.

Other Books by Belinda Vasquez Garcia

Novels

Return of the Bones

The Witch Narratives Reincarnation
(Land of Enchantment Trilogy 1)

Ghosts of the Black Rose
(Land of Enchantment Trilogy 2)

Rise of the Black Rose
(Land of Enchantment Trilogy 3)

Author Website
http://belindavasquezgarcia.com

Chapter 1:1

So man built twin ladders to try to reach heaven,
But the devil ripped the ladders from the earth
And scattered the ashes above Manhattan.
And all the mayor's horses and all the mayor's men
Could never put the Twin Towers back together again.

Thursday, September 20, 2001

The last person Miranda expected to see in the rubble of Ground Zero was—*Jake! Oh, my God, you're alive!* She dropped the poster of her brother printed from MissingAtWorldTradeCenter.com.

Jake leaned against a damaged railing, smoke billowing around him. He reached out a hand to her.

I must go to him. Maybe he's hurt. She bent to crawl under the yellow tape.

Jake slowly faded, vanishing into dusty air.

She heard footsteps running down the stairs of the World Trade Center (WTC) Subway Station—the red line, Cortlandt Street.

"Jake, come back!" she screamed.

"Over here. I think I hear something. Over here," a
rescuer
yelled. It was the spot where Jake had been standing.

She gripped her stomach.

Men dug, seeking life beneath pulverized steel, concrete, and gypsum. Sweat poured from their faces. Muscles bulged beneath their shirts. If will alone could resurrect life from the ashes, there would be no one missing at Ground Zero.

Rescuers dug until their arms hung limp at their sides.

Miranda shoved her way through the crowd to a rescue worker wearing an FDNY uniform. He shook his shaggy head, drank a bottle of water, and cleared his throat.

"I saw my brother," she said in a winded voice.

"You're white as a sheet, Lady. You okay," he said in a thick New Jersey accent.

"He was over there." She pointed to the subway station

The tall, heavy-set rescuer rocked on his boots. "Your brother should not be crossing the yellow tape. He could get hurt down there."

"Jake is one of the missing from the South Tower."

"I'm confused—you said you just saw him."

"I did, and he disappeared. Then I heard him running down the subway stairs."

"Now, now," he said, patting her arm awkwardly. "When people are hurting, they see strange things. I hear stories about sinister images rising from the ashes. Faces of the devil were seen in the black clouds, after the planes hit the Towers. There are shapes of crosses all over the site, some real, some seen only by the observer. But you are a first for me," he said, shaking his head, his eyes filled with pity.

"Maybe Jake was on the subway that morning," she said.

"The operator found out in time and diverted the train," he said in a soothing voice.

"Maybe my brother was in the area of the subway station. Search for him," she said, clutching his sleeve tighter.

"I told you, we dug down there."

"Jake is trying to communicate with me. You've got to search the subway!"

He looked at her like she was crazy.

"Please," she whispered.

He gave a heartfelt sigh. "We'll search there again. What's your name, Missy?"

She took a deep breath. "My name is Miranda Balboa."

"In the meantime, Miranda, I suggest you talk to a grief counselor. Do this for your brother. I'm sure Jake, wherever he is, wouldn't like to see you so upset."

"You promise to look?" she said, working her fingers beneath his glove. She pinched his wrist with her nails, and he grimaced.

"I promise we'll look over the area," he said, tiredly.

"Thank you," she whispered.

"We'll do all we can to find your brother. Now go," he said, pointing to where grief counselors were lined up.

He hollered at fellow rescuers to search the subway section again.

Miranda felt on her head for her sunglasses, but they were lost. *No place to hide,* she thought and wandered listlessly towards a clinical-looking corner of men and women in white coats. Would a grief counselor label her insane about seeing Jake? Not all of the Twin Towers vaporized on September 11th after being rammed by two commercial jets piloted by terrorists. There were still puzzles of skyscraper parts at Ground Zero and air pockets, which might sustain life. *Jake must be trapped.*

Once again, Jake materialized. He stood on the top subway stair with his arms crossed.

This time, she could see right through him to a steel picket fence a mere five stories tall. The Twin Towers had been 110 stories in height.

Jake walked slowly back down the subway stairs, turning to give her a final look.

She waved, but he faded into the stairway walls.

"Come back to me, Jake. Just please, wherever you are, hang on," she mumbled.

Suddenly, a man grabbed her arms and shook her. "Are you okay? You look like you've seen a ghost."

"Insensitive jerk! Ground Zero is not the place to be mentioning ghosts," she said and kicked him.

He grimaced and held her tighter, whispering into her ear, "It is said that if one dies a violent death, his ghost will haunt the place which holds his name."

"Let go of me, you brute," she said, twisting her arms from the grievance counselor.

"I'm the brute? You're the one who kicked me, Lady!"

She butted her head against his broad chest, but he still did not release her.

"You win. I concede you're stronger. Now let me go," she said.

He shoved her so she almost fell. He defiantly stared with a grim look in his grayish eyes which roamed the top of her head and slid down her cheekbones, high on her fragile, soft-looking face. Looks can be deceiving. She had been mistaken. This man was not an insensitive jerk. He looked at her with such empathy, as if he, too, saw her missing brother haunting the WTC remains.

Don't be foolish. The good doctor looks at everyone at Ground Zero the way he's looking at you. He has reason to. We're all emotional wrecks, she thought.

"I've changed my mind about therapy," she stammered.

"You have, huh? You're as nervous as a wound-up bunny," he said in a voice used to calm horses.

"Treatment is my prerogative," she snapped.

"Yeah, I guess you can change your mind," he said in a laughing voice. The creep thought she was funny.

He stepped back, raising his hands peacefully.

"This is still a free country," she said. "The terrorists have not taken that from us." Miranda walked away with her arms held stiff at her sides.

From the corner of her eye she watched the grievance counselor. He stood where she abandoned him, waving half-heartedly.

"Go help a shell-shocked survivor," she mouthed at him.

He smiled to the side of his mouth, a lightning smile.

She gave him a dirty look.

From seemingly out of nowhere, a dog scratched at her legs. The pathetic creature was a scraggly Shih Tzu. The little guy was irresistible with enormous brown eyes peeping beneath a mop of ash-streaked fur.

She scooped the dog into her arms.

Its owner was nowhere around.

"Look at you," she said.

The dog smiled at her.

"You must have been playing at Ground Zero. Don't you know you shouldn't, Scamp? The rescue worker said no fooling around. This is serious stuff. You could get hurt."

The dog licked her face. His fur was charcoaled.

"You look just like an ash pile."

She buried her face in the dog, inhaling the stench of scorched fur and ashes. The Shih Tzu smelled like Ground Zero, and Miranda finally released her dam of tears. She squeezed her eyes shut and could see an image of Flight 175 approaching the South Tower, and Jake sitting at his desk, sipping coffee, settling in for the work day.

Miranda cried until she had no more tears. She hiccupped with her face buried in the dog's fur.

She swore she heard singing:

Grim Reaper,
Death's Keeper,
How does your garden grow?
With senseless terror,
Misguided destruction,
And collapsed buildings all in a row.

§

Chapter 2:1

And beneath the devastation
Shall dwell a world all its own.

The lost little dog she named Ashes had five dry-urinating episodes. Who knows how long he was lost. The dog drank a bottle of water from a Styrofoam bowl like he was putting out a fire.

Miranda hired a taxi parked at the curb. "The Algonquin Hotel on 44th Street," she said to the driver.

She mindlessly stared out the cab window. Chills crawled up her spine—s*omeone is staring at me.*

Miranda twisted her head around to the cab behind and sucked in her breath. The shape of a man, shadow-like and faceless rode in the back seat.

"Go around the block and then stop at the hotel," she instructed the driver of her taxi.

Miranda sighed with relief when the other cab didn't follow.

The light must have made the passenger seem like a ghost. Ground Zero has me jittery.

Miranda sat in her cab at the Algonquin, wondering if she should go to a police station. She still couldn't shake the sense someone was watching her. She tensely looked around at other taxis in the area.

The police will think I'm insane if all I have is a creepy feeling. Do I tell them a sinister ghost is following me, or a shadow from Ground Zero? Well, I can't sit in this cab all evening, like a frightened school girl.

She paid the cabbie and wrapped Ashes in her sweater. Miranda whispered in the dog's ear, "Sh. Keep quiet. Tomorrow, I'll try and find your owner, see if someone's advertised. Sorry about having to hide you, but the hotel doesn't allow pets, except for the resident cat."

Ashes wagged his tail.

She scratched her sweater where his head was buried. "I'm sorry that's all I can do for you, Ashes, but the city is big."

Manhattan is too big, she thought, scanning the cabs in the vicinity. It was getting dark and all the taxis had ghostly shadows sitting in the back seats.

Hiss!

Her heart nearly jumped out of her chest. "Hello, Hamlet. Nice kitty," she said, clamping her hand over Ashes' nose and chin.

The long-haired, white cat with gray face and legs stepped from behind the concierge, raising its fur and spitting.

"I don't know what's wrong with her, Miss," the concierge said. "She usually takes to everyone."

Miranda scurried to the elevator, pushing the button to the twelfth floor. Ashes poked his nose out of her sweater while they rode to her room.

Their dinner arrived with a knock at the door.

Ashes hid under the bed. Only his eyes were showing.

"Good boy," she murmured.

Her mouth was bone-dry, tasting like she swallowed a cup of Ground Zero. Miranda wiped her cheek. She cringed at the gray dust on her napkin—a bit of the Twin Towers. All who went to Ground Zero carried away specks of the fallen skyscrapers—and ghosts?

I must have imagined Jake at Ground Zero because I desperately long to see him. My brother is missing, not dead. The reporter said so when he flashed his poster across the screen, asking if anyone had seen Jacob Balbo. I'm still looking for my long, lost brother, she thought. *I've been searching for Jake half my life.*

Miranda glued her chocolate-colored eyes to a copy of Jake's missing poster. He was smiling, his skin stretched across his facial bones, making him look as tightly wound as a drum. He wore faded blue jeans with a hole in one knee. His rumpled shirttail hung half-way down his thighs

His eyebrow was raised and he seemed to be saying, *did you miss me, Mandy?*

Of course I did, Jake.

How long has it been since Social Services separated us after Mom and Dad died?

Thirteen years. How odd that you moved to New York City.

The Big Apple was a place Miranda vacationed to. It was possible they breathed the same air during her visits. Perhaps they passed each other on the street. Maybe she walked in one door of Macy's and he walked out the other door. She even once toured the WTC where a startup named Egghead Revolution listed Jake as missing after the 9/11 attacks and posted his picture across the news channels. She had been at home in Los Angeles when the news flashed the photo of a man with her brother's name. He was the spitting image of her deceased father.

The little dog now jumped on the remote, turning off the newsreel that was repeatedly playing a clip of the falling Twin Towers. Ashes lay with his head on his paws, whining.

Miranda bathed the dog in the tub, washing him with hotel-flowery-smelling shampoo and coconut conditioner. She closed the shower curtain in order to rinse the shampoo off Ashes.

The shower valve moved by itself, spraying her face.

Damn ancient hotel and faulty plumbing, she thought.

The dog stood obediently while she blew his fur with a hair dryer. When she ran her hand across his back, his fur felt like ashes. He still smelled like fire. Ashes didn't look very clean. It was as if Ground Zero clung to him.

"It will take more than one bath to get the filth of Ground Zero from you, mister."

Ashes barked as if he agreed with her. He jumped on the bed.

She placed him on the floor, examining the bedspread. "Well, you're not contagious. I don't see any ash."

She stripped off her clothes, looking forward to a hot shower.

Now the frickin' shower head kept turning itself off.

Miranda shuffled into the bedroom, leaned back against the headboard, and mindlessly watched television for about twenty minutes until the news came on.

A smiling anchor woman, safe and smug behind the camera, announced, "The rescue operation at Ground Zero is now a recovery operation. It's been nine days since the tragedy. The mayor..."

Miranda threw the remote at the set and crawled beneath the covers. The expression "recovery operation" made her shudder.

The dog's thumping tail on her thigh was comforting, like a heart beating.

Crap, the maid tucked the sheet in too tightly.

Great! Now the sheet entangled her ankles.

Brr! It's freezing. Turn up the heat.

Christ, it's hot! Lower the thermostat.

The room kept going from hot to cold and vice-versa.

Miranda blew at her bangs, her forehead damp with sweat. Chills dotted her calves.

A light snoring came from Ashes but—someone breathed between his snores.

I checked under the bed and behind the shower curtain. Besides, this big strong dog is beside me. Miranda nervously laughed at the little lump on the bed that was Ashes.

Hold your breath! Make sure it isn't you.

Miranda sucked in her breath, and the husky breathing stopped. *It was me I heard breathing.* She giggled then cringed at a crinkling noise.

She yanked the covers over her head. "One. Two Three," she whispered, counting to one hundred. She peeked out from the covers.

A door creaked.

Where's the lamp switch? Oh, fu…

She snapped on the lamp.

Door closed.

Chain lock in place.

Dead bolt turned.

Ah, good! The dead bolt is, also, locked on the door adjoining my room with a stranger's room.

Miranda tiptoed to the bathroom and slammed her hand against the light switch. Thinking about Norman Bates in *Psycho*, she slid open the shower curtain and nearly fell in the tub.

She flicked off the lights, crawled back in bed and tried to relax.

The television kept turning on by itself, just like the bathroom fixtures earlier.

Remembering that her garage door opened and closed by itself when the battery was going dead on the remote control, Miranda removed the batteries from the remote. She turned off the TV and tried to fall asleep.

The television flashed on. 9/11 new s blared from the set, the volume rising and lowering by itself.

"Shitty, faulty electrical!" Miranda jerked the cord from the outlet.

At least the mattress isn't an antique like the rest of the hotel, she thought before closing her eyes.

Miranda fell in love with New York City on her first visit, but could never get used to the noise. Even from the closed windows of her room, twelve stories high, she could hear the clanking of a subway train. Tonight, she took comfort in a subway train grinding its brakes and then the train screeching when it took off.

And so Miranda finally slept, and she dreamed...

Of a midnight world where time stood still at Ground Zero. At the entrance of the WTC Subway Station a red globe spun, making a grinding noise atop a red-white-and-blue barber shop pole.

The red ball glowed and dimmed continuously.

Fog rolled up the stairs leading down to the terminal and swirled about the subway railing.

The fog moved towards Miranda, encircling her ankles to her knees.

The cloud whirled like a tornado up her body, blowing her hair in her eyes.

The fog cleared and she gasped at Jake.

Her brother chewed his bottom lip in the manner he always did when indecisive.

Jake, we have so much to say, thirteen years to catch up on, she mouthed.

He brushed her shoulder and ran down the stairs to the subway.

Miranda chased after him, her steps pounding against the twisting metal steps. She ran down, down to the dimly lit station.

Entry turnstiles lined up like metal guards, blocking her way to the subway.

Jake's footsteps grew fainter.

She would sell her soul for a subway token.

No need. Someone left a one-way MetroCard propped up at the unmanned agent's booth. The subway ticket was for Train Zero, traveling on the Red Line, Z, the end of the line—one way, no going back. She would catch that train, if it meant seeing Jake, so Miranda pushed her hip against the squealing turnstile.

Her shoes made a hollow sound as she ran down the stairs leading to the trains.

The station was deserted. It was midnight—not a good time to be trapped in the New York Subway.

But this station, the WTC Station, was not ratty looking like the others. The terminal was surreal. The WTC Station looked brand new, the way it must have when first built, before would-be poets and artists scribbled profanity, anger and comedy on the walls. The station even smelled like a newborn babe, of baby powder and lotion. Gone was the human garbage stink the NYC Subway is famous for. There were no regurgitated meals, undigested drinks, or next-morning stench of cheap winos. The air smelled fresh without the suffocating odor of exhaust fumes, or the electrical aroma of trains stopping and taking off.

The station walls waved, giving an illusion that the train across from her was moving on the tracks. The train wobbled sideways, never going forward, stuck forever at the WTC Station.

Jake looked out a window, the lone passenger on the train. Ashes sat on his lap, the dog's tongue hanging out.

But they were not alone—Miranda felt someone else's presence.

Something brushed past her, the slightest touch of a hand.

There was a sigh but no one was in sight.

She heard whisperings and sniffed the odor of peppermint mouthwash.

She spun. No one was there. Yet, someone stared at Miranda, making her squirm with the feeling that she was being undressed.

Miranda covered her chest with her arms, hiding her breasts.

She gasped, showing her back to the invisible person leering at her. The ghost smelled of cool aftershave, the odor of Old Spice cologne, like a man just returned from the sea.

Meanwhile, Jake climbed the train ladder.

Show off!

He danced along the top of the train.

Don't. You'll get hurt, Jake, she yelled at him. What if the train takes off?

Her dead parents appeared beside Miranda. They stared at the train, their faces white and eyes unmoving.

Mama, look at Jake. See what's he's doing. Stop him, Daddy! Tell him to get down. Please, stop him!

Her mother and father did not say a word to Miranda. They held hands and walked away, vanishing after a few steps.

Miranda jumped off the subway platform, running along the tracks to reach her brother.

She tripped and fell into the tracks.

Ouch. That hurt like hell. Her foot was wedged in the track railing, her ankle swelling. She pulled, pushed and twisted but could not free her foot.

She gritted her teeth, massaging her ankle.

From out of nowhere, roared the sound of an approaching train. The headlight was blinding.

She tried to rise but her foot, goddamn her foot! Damn the railing. Damn. Damn.

Crap! The train was coming closer, the wheels grinding against the rails as it traveled straight at her.

The train kept coming, and she opened her mouth to scream, but her vocal chords were frozen. Her head was rattling against the rails and the heat from the tracks was unbearable.

Oh, my God! The train is going to behead me!

Her legs were under the passing train.

Now her chest!

Bam!

Miranda was jolted back to the real world. Her body was numb from sleep, except for her lungs which hurt to breathe with such a tight chest. She gasped shocking, cold air. Sweat poured between her breasts. Her lashes were soaked and her lids swollen.

"What…what's that? Who's there?" she mumbled.

The bed creaked.

Her heart slammed against her ribs.

The mattress sagged from a heavy weight, rolling her towards the left side of the bed.

A hand reached beneath the sheet, grasped her calf and squeezed.

§

Chapter 3:1

And terror will crawl beneath the skin.

A man's large shadow sat on the bed, the smell of his after-shave filling the room. Old Spice, just like the ghost in her dream.

Wake up, Mandy! Wake up! Wake up, she silently ordered but couldn't stir from her frozen state. She was half-awake and half-dreaming with the sensation that the man spied on her while she slept, exposed and vulnerable.

Wake up, Mandy! Wake up!

The man sighed deeply and his breath smelled like peppermint mouthwash.

God save me from a rapist or robber! Or a murderer!

He leaned over her.

Wake up, Mandy, she commanded

herself.

He chuckled, amused by her antics.

She tossed her head across the pillow, rocking her body on the sheet.

Wake up! Goddamn it, wake up completely!

Her uninvited guest shifted his weight from her left side, to the end of the mattress.

Wake up, Miranda! Wake!

She fluttered her eyelids.

The room was engulfed in a hazy light.

A brighter light glowed at the end of the bed.

Miranda sunk lower into the mattress.

The light touched her hair—a ghost smelling of Old Spice, coffee, peppermint mouthwash, and a pine coffin.

The light wiggled restlessly. "Mandy", was spoken faintly into her ear.

"Jake?" she murmured. Only Jake had ever called her Mandy.

The room darkened as full consciousness swirled around her.

Footsteps ran lightly across the carpet.

A door closed.

Miranda fumbled for the light switch. There was no one in the room but her and the sleeping Ashes. Throughout all her drama, Ashes slept peacefully, still snoring as if the dog didn't have a care in the world. His little body was toasty warm.

The doors were still locked. Miranda appeared safe and sound. Nothing frightening was in her room but her own racing mind, and a cramp in her leg hurting like hell. Miranda massaged her calf, wishing she could have brought her gun with her. The class she had enjoyed the most and excelled at all through high school was ROTC. She once seriously considered joining the military and now wished that she was a bad-ass soldier.

If there was a ghost in my room, Ashes would have barked. Dogs can sense the supernatural. I just had one of those dreams where it feels like you're awake.

Miranda stumbled into the bathroom.

Her ghastly face stared back from the mirror— big eyes looking scared; hair sticking up as if she'd seen a ghost; full lips bloody with teeth marks; thick, curly lashes glistening with tears and cheeks sunken into her face bones.

Miranda plopped on the toilet seat, and blew her nose into a roll of toilet paper. She wrapped her arms around her waist and rocked.

"The rescue operation at Ground Zero is now a recovery operation," the newswoman had reported.

That annoying man had whispered into her ear: It is said that if one dies a violent death, his ghost will haunt the place that holds his name.

The Twin Towers had been filled with offices of men and women, their names proudly mounted on doors, cubicles and desks—possibly her brother's name. Miranda closed her eyes, imagining Jake walking into the South Tower elevator, the building crashing down and...

She swallowed a few aspirin, washing them down with a glass of water that splashed about her shaky hand.

The glass slipped through her fingers, crashing to the tile—*I really did see Jake's ghost earlier at Ground Zero. His apparition was not a figment of my imagination.*

Jake can't be dead! He was trying to contact me. It was not his ghost I saw but some other manifestation of his spirit. He's trapped at Ground Zero.

Miranda tiptoed around shards of glass in the bathroom, making her way to the plush carpet of her room, and the warmth of the bed. She cradled the tissue box, just in case.

She wrapped the blankets around her like a mummy. The bed was like ice.

The clock blared out two a.m.

She tossed and turned, but still the clock ticked loudly.

Three a.m.

Four a.m.

Five a.m.

Six a.m.

§

Chapter 4:1

And mistrust will reign.

Friday, September 21, 2001

Miranda placed an ad in the *New York Times* on behalf of Ashes. She ran a brush through her unruly black hair, and then rode the elevator to the lobby.

The staff in the Round Table Room stumbled all over themselves to please her with jams, rolls and coffee. New York waiters were no longer snotty like before 9/11 but acted kindly.

Miranda lifted a glass of orange juice to her mouth and the hair rose at the nape of her neck—a man stared intently at her.

Him.

The grievance counselor from yesterday. The tall, golden, Viking-looking man with home-butchered hair brushing his shoulders and an odd sense of humor. If she told him about Jake's ghost and her dream, he would probably laugh out loud.

The man was perhaps still angry because she kicked him.

The counselor must have followed me to the hotel yesterday. Maybe there was no ghost in my room last night. Her stomach cramped at this thought. The threat of a live invader in her room, watching her sleep, frightened her more than ghosts. The living was scarier than the dead.

The guy totally creeps me out. He was maybe thirty or so, unshaven and grubby looking.

He tapped a weather-beaten wallet against the table, his face appearing indecisive. He narrowed his eyes at her and then at his wallet. He twisted his head back and forth in this manner, several gut-wrenching times.

Does he think me a prostitute who can be bought with money?

He slapped the wallet back in his pants.

Last night in my room there was an intruder she thought. Her breath caught in her throat when he slid his chair from the table, rising to his superior height. Miranda glanced nervously at him, but he would never know it since she wore a new pair of sunglasses, preventing eye contact with anyone. Eye contact meant involvement. Involvement led to listening to meaningless chatter of passing strangers. Miranda mostly hid behind a façade of reserved coolness, except with the children she taught. With children she could be herself. Miranda joked and laughed and tried to please. She could trust a child, but never a man.

His strong jaw tightened, revealing his disapproval. Similar looks had crushed her—a dozen sets of foster parents complained she was too smart for her own good and willful.

A navy-blue turtleneck swallowed his noble head. This morning, he looked more like a poor college student than a grief counselor. More like a casual rapist than a formal one. More like a man who killed for sport rather than for business.

Hold on there. I wasn't killed or raped last night, not even close. Besides, I don't know for sure if I'm being stupid or delusional.

"Hello. Hello again," he said in his deep, sexy New-York voice sounding like it came from inside the Lincoln Tunnel. He rocked on his feet in front of her table. In one hand he balanced a cup and saucer, his other hand shoved deep into his pants' pocket. He smelled of alcohol. It was early to be drinking. He stood unsteady, and his bloodshot eyes kept closing, like he might pass out.

She came right to the point. "Are you stalking me?"

He rubbed his ear, playing with his earlobe.

Maybe it was a nervous gesture. There was something about him decidedly different. His confrontational manner of yesterday was absent. His superior attitude, that he knew what was best for her, was replaced by a confused look—probably from booze.

"If you mean, am I also staying in this hotel, the answer is nope," he said with a slight slur in his voice. He set his cup and saucer carefully on her table, as if the cup might spill. His cup was empty. "There now," he said, tapping the saucer.

He slid out a chair, swinging it around and straddling it, with the chairback against his chest. "I come here all the time to eat. The food's pretty good," he said, rubbing his chin across the top of the chair. "My name by the way is Christopher. Christopher Michaels."

Miranda stared back in chilly silence.

He seemed restless, like a caged animal about to pounce.

He rolled his eyes, looking around the mostly-empty restaurant, which before the September 11th attack would have been full to the brim with tourists. "We may as well sit together so the wait staff doesn't have to work so hard. If we're to be breakfast companions, I should know your name, Miss...?"

"I'm not in need of your expensive services," she snapped.

He leaned towards her, grinning. "Actually, my services are free," he said in a husky voice.

She gave him a dirty look and concentrated on her omelet.

He coughed into his hand. "You're a tough nut to crack."

"I'm not crazy!"

"If you do come to your senses and feel like talking, here's my cell phone number." He took a pen from his jacket and with hands shaking like an alcoholic, scribbled his contact information on a napkin in bold black numbers. He folded the napkin, placing it in the pocket of her jacket hanging on the chair.

"Well then," he said, standing with his arms hanging limp. He hesitated, like he waited for her to ask him to stay.

She shoveled eggs in her mouth, chewing the yolk like it was sawdust.

"Bye, Princess," he mumbled.

"Fuck," she heard him mutter as he turned to leave.

His table was set for one. Michaels had not ordered breakfast nor even drank a cup of coffee. *He probably drinks his breakfast,* she thought, meanly. Indeed, he zigzagged his way from the restaurant, leaving behind a strong odor of whiskey.

She jumped from her seat, discretely following to make sure he really left.

He nearly tripped over Ashes where the dog was tied up outside the hotel.

Miranda signaled Ashes with her eyes and teeth to bite him.

The dog, surprisingly, had revealed a vicious nature. Ashes growled and snapped at everyone who walked by him, except for Michaels, who stooped down to pet a dog so obviously happy to see him, like a long-lost buddy.

Traitor, she thought.

Ashes lifted his paws to his knees, licking him across the face.

He's a bossy man.

Michaels held his hand out, ordering Ashes to stay.

Ashes lowered his head and whined, acting like he would rather go with him.

Michaels whispered into the dog's ear and then walked away, whistling a bawdy tune, with his hands in his pockets.

Michaels spun, looking straight at her.

Miranda darted into the hotel with her heart beating fast and her palms sweating.

§

Chapter 5:1

And truth will be revealed
When rescue becomes recovery.

Holding her breath, Miranda placed her foot on the 44th Street sidewalk and dove into the crowd with her arms smashed against her sides and her head bowed. Only a people junkie could love living in Manhattan with so many people cramped into such a small amount of vertical real estate. When she passed people on the street, Miranda felt as if she could taste their breakfast, which made her queasy. She was not used to being this close to strangers, and took deep breaths to keep from drowning.

The walkers shoved Miranda towards Ground Zero, the scene of the mother of all crimes. Despite her nightmare of last night, she wasn't prepared for the site striking her again, like an arrow through her heart.

She fell to her knees, joining others mingling around the yellow tape. Some prayed with serene faces to a skeleton wall of a cathedral-like shape of steel strips teetering in the debris. Sunlight glowed through the strips.

Ashes stared at the rubble of the Twin Towers as if the dog was in a trance.

Miranda wiped her eyes with the backs of her hands. She sniffled against her glove, chewing on the leather. *The rescue operation at Ground Zero is now a recovery operation.* Any hope of finding life in the rubble was officially abandoned.

She blindly reached out a hand. *Hang on, Jake, please, hang on. Oh, God, how can I find you, only to lose you again? This could not have happened.*

If one dies a violent death, his ghost will haunt the place that holds his name—she couldn't keep this thought out of her head.

The ghosts are restless. They don't know what's happened to them.

Miranda closed her eyes, listening to garbled voices coming from beneath the ground and whispers from crowded stairwells, the ghosts unaware the stairs no longer existed. She heard heavy breathing from running down so many flights of stairs, and hearts pumping in fear like trapped animals, their adrenaline jumping off the charts.

I only imagine hearing ghosts. My dream from last night makes me jittery and brings back memories of my brother. She could hear Jake's voice when they were little—Mandy, look at you. You fell and skinned your knee. Didn't I tell you not to ride my new bike? That you'd get hurt. You're too little. You can barely reach the brakes.

Jake can't be dead, she thought with disbelief.

The last time Miranda saw her brother was the day after their parent's funeral. Their youth was highjacked by a drunk driver, leaving Mandy and Jake with nowhere to go but foster homes. Brother and sister were ripped apart. At the age of ten, she lost her entire family. Jake had been eleven.

Miranda yanked out a picture of her father from her purse, holding it up to the missing poster. Yup. The two pictures were nearly identical. This Jacob Balboa had to be her brother Jake. Her brother's hair was reddish-brown, unlike her midnight-colored hair, but there was a resemblance between them, the curve of their lips and their expressive eyes.

When their parents died, Jake said, "Don't cry, Mandy. I'll make it better. I promise I will." Jake never made good on his promise. She lost him long ago. All these years after their parents' deaths, her brother was simply a dream.

Jake. Oh, God, Jake.

Someone tapped her shoulder and Miranda jumped. *Jake,* she thought, her heart thumping.

"We share a common loss," a deep, familiar voice said from behind her.

His breath crowned the top of her head, and she could smell alcohol. *Why isn't the jerk at work counseling people?*

She turned around, expecting to see Christopher Michaels, a man with a unique voice, sounding like it came from inside a tunnel.

"Are you going to run from me again?" he said, his square jaw tense.

She gave him the silent treatment.

"Did you hear me?" he said loudly, like she was deaf. "We both know Balboa."

Right. So he knows Jake. She had been holding the printout with her brother's name on it. Michaels had looked over her shoulder like a turkey, gobbling to himself that she was alone. He was spying on her and taking advantage. She was an outsider, a lone female in the big, bad city filled with wolves and other predators. There was a chill in the air—coming from him.

Yesterday, he grabs me.

Last night…maybe he was in my room.

This morning, he appears out of nowhere at the Algonquin, pulls out a beaten wallet, doesn't order any food, so he's probably broke. He doesn't appear to have a job.

Now this. All too much of a coincidence. Is he after sex or money?

Her eyes boldly roamed Michaels from head to toe, trying to make him feel as uncomfortable as she. He must have grown warm and removed his turtleneck. He wore a V-neck T-shirt, and the top bones of his chest were showing. His pulse beat rapidly on his broad neck. His shoe tapped against the concrete as though waiting for these preliminaries to be over so he could drag her behind the nearest building and ravage her.

"I said I know Jacob," he slowly repeated as if she was retarded.

The pity in his eyes could be deceiving, just like his seductive voice, still sounding like it came from inside a tunnel.

Looks can create an illusion and be deceptive, just like her soft appearance, masking a toughness of growing up in foster homes and serving time in a juvenile detention facility.

She itched to punch his face and wipe that smirk off. He was smug, conceited and oh so sure of himself. Michaels didn't fool her for a second. He believed she was an easy pickup. Miranda may be a woman on her own in New York City but was certainly no fool. I know Jacob, he had said.

Right, Sherlock. I bet you know Jake. It doesn't take a detective to figure you out. Yesterday, you single me out. This morning, you waltz into the Round Room nosing around, hoping I would be eating breakfast. Now, you take advantage of my missing brother—here at Ground Zero, for heaven's sake. Prick! I should rub Jake's name in your face.

Instead, Miranda lowered her boot. She never punched a man in public, especially a stranger. Oh, she used to brawl at bars, but she was more respectful of Ground Zero than this butthead.

She blew her breath out, the feathery feel of her bangs across her forehead refreshing. *Calm down. Calm down. One. Two. Three.* She nervously laughed, brushing her bangs from her forehead.

After thinking I saw Jake yesterday and my dream of last night, for a moment I could have sworn I didn't hear Michael's footsteps approach. He frightened me, sneaking behind my back. Ground Zero is filled with ghosts.

It seems we share a common loss, he claims. He has no idea.

She twirled, daggers flying from her eyes. "Yes I did hear you. What a lot of nerve it takes, Mister, preying on the tragedy of others. Your pickup line is original if not despicable," she said, gripping her hands to keep them from battering his chest. *Oh, my God! I just spoke boldly in a bitchy tone to such a savage looking man.*

He smiled at her with his mouth to one side, more grimace than smile. His smile never reached his cold gray eyes. "I never meant to scare you but, Lady, you try my patience." He took a deep breath. "I'm attempting to be kinder since September 11th. Like most New Yorkers, Black Tuesday has changed me, but old habits die hard. Before the fall of the Twin Towers, I was an arrogant asshole, but I made a vow. I am Jacob's friend. I know who you are. I know he grew up in Austin," he said more gently. "Jacob had no family except for a sister he was forcibly separated from. Mandy?"

Jake had been the only one who ever called her Mandy, not even her parents.

"They said I could call you and I will, Mandy. I promise. Someday we'll be together again. Just you and me. Just you and me."

With her arms outstretched she had run after the car carrying her brother away.

Jake plastered his face against the back windshield, screaming.

Miranda spent months sitting by phones that never rang.

When she turned eighteen, she searched for Jake with desperation, eventually turning to acceptance that she might never see her brother again, and was alone in the world.

Miranda flew nearly three thousand miles to find out the truth, but still could not fully accept that the Jacob Balboa on the printout was really her brother because if she believed this, it would mean that...that...

Michaels said we share a common loss.

Jake's dead. For sure, for certain. Forever.

Dead was her last thought before Miranda fainted.

§

Chapter 6:1

No matter how painful,
No matter how hard,
A veil will be lifted.

A hand softly rubbed her cheek and a sing-song voice said, "Wake up, Mandy. Wake up. Wake up."

A light sprinkling of silky hair tickled her cheek. Her new sunglasses had fallen from her face, and the sun was so bright. *Get hold of yourself, Mandy. Don't you dare cry in front of him!*

"You look so damned vulnerable," he muttered, obviously thinking she was still in la-la land. He stroked her cheek and his gentleness nearly undid her. "Mandy?"

Using her nickname threatened to shatter her composure. Her chest fell and rose slowly, painfully.

"Good. I'm glad you're alive. For a minute there, you seemed lifeless," he said his eyes bleak. "You don't look much like Jacob Balboa. I never would have picked you out of the crowd as his sister. Your brother described you as sweet but you seem more like a rebel."

She hadn't been sweet since she was ten years old and her parents died. She gritted her teeth, determined to hide her shyness behind her mask of toughness. "I am Miranda Balboa," she said, wondering how he turned the tables on her so she was assuring him she was Jake's sister.

"I'll give you the benefit of the doubt," he said, grunting.

"Oh, shall I show you my driver's license then?" she said sarcastically

"Heaven forbid," he said, shuddering.

"You really knew Jake?" she said in a small voice, hoping he would contradict her and say—I just came from a local bar where Jake's waiting to celebrate your reunion.

"I know…knew Jake," he said, appearing flustered and confused.

Ground Zero is now a recovery operation. Of course! Through this man, Miranda could recover her lost brother and by doing so, perhaps find herself, the carefree girl she had once been, the winner who didn't screw up, the girl once filled with dreams. For years Miranda had not allowed herself to fantasize about Jake and what sort of man he had become.

I know Balboa, he had said.

His words crawled inside her, blowing hope in her ear that she might still find Jake, even though he was dead. She closed her eyes, envisioning a recurring dream of one day walking down the street, and there in front of her would be Jake, smiling at her with his hands held out. Michaels must know about her brother's life.

All she could do now was search for her brother's past. There were 13 missing years between them. Jake's life was in Manhattan. Perhaps Michaels knew where he had lived, who his neighbors were, and where he walked on his daily travels around town.

"Are you okay now?" Michaels said in a guarded voice, still grasping her hand in his.

His hand was rough and blistered with ragged cuticles. Dirt was caked beneath his fingernails, which were scuffed and worn, like he had been scratching and digging. She examined every line on his hand, like a blind woman softly strumming her fingers over him as if he was an instrument she was learning to play.

His breathing changed, his eyes lightening to a silvery gray. "Are you a palm reader?" he said in a husky voice.

She dropped his hand.

His jaw tightened.

She suddenly noticed he was sitting on the sidewalk, cradling her head in his lap. His left arm encircled her shoulders and her breast brushed his arm.

She sat up—too quickly. Skyscrapers spun around her.

He stood, crunching her sunglasses beneath his shoe.

She winced but said nothing.

He picked up the poster and stared at her brother's picture with intense pain.

Miranda choked on the apology she was about to make for fainting in his arms.

Michaels gave the missing poster of Jake back to her.

Their fingers touched, causing sparks of static electricity to vibrate through her. Instead of relinquishing the paper, he hauled her to her feet.

She was inexplicably disappointed when he let go of her hand.

He buried his fists in his pockets, his face guarded.

Miranda hated seeming weak. "Thanks. If you had not caught me, I would have hit my head," she said.

"It might have knocked some sense into you," he muttered.

"So, you really did know Jake?"

"I do. Did. I did know him. Yeah. That's right," he said, clearing his throat. "Sorry for freaking you out with this mess. They don't usually let me out of my cubicle."

"You didn't scare me," she said with false bravado in her voice.

"Then why are you so pale?" he said, raising an eyebrow.

"Well, it's just..." She shrugged her shoulders.

"Yes?"

"When you tapped me on the back, I thought you were a ghost," she mumbled.

"A ghost?" he said, widening his eyes.

If he laughs at me, I'll curl up like a cockroach.

Emotion swirled around his gray eyes, softening his orbs to a smoky color. "I should never have made that stupid comment yesterday about ghosts, but you're kidding, right? Right?" he said in such a gentle voice she felt like confessing her life story to him, including the nicks and cuts.

Miranda shook her head no, that she wasn't kidding about ghosts. "This place is haunted," she whispered.

"Haunted? You're right. These good folks keep returning every day. They mean well, I suppose," he said, frowning.

"And how about you? I've see you every time I've come to Ground Zero," she said.

"I guess I'm haunting the fallen South Tower. I can't seem to help myself," he said in a somber voice.

"Why the South Tower?"

He hesitated before saying, "I used to work there."

"I thought you were a doctor or therapist giving pep talks, and prescribing numbing drugs for grief or stress, all followed by appointments at your more conventional office."

"You're my only patient. I'm here to fix you," he said, winking. How confusing since he earlier claimed—they don't usually let me out of my cubicle. Doctors have offices. He looked down at the ground, avoiding her eyes.

She assumed that like most men, he didn't care to watch a woman cry, but after shamelessly fainting, the last thing Miranda wanted to do was sob in front of him. An uncomfortable moment passed between them.

She broke the ice. "I meant Ground Zero might be haunted by men and women who died at this place. Do you think their spirits are here, among us?"

"I guess if one believes in ghosts and fairy tales, and all that scary crap."

"You said yesterday that if one dies a violent death, his ghost will haunt the place that holds his name. If that's true, then nearly 3,000 ghosts could haunt Ground Zero."

"I was talking bullshit. I was in a dark place yesterday. Okay, so I was hung-over and drunk on my ass. Don't pay attention to a man who drinks," he said his eyes still bloodshot.

He was in a dark place yesterday? His face was drawn and pale, like he'd just been to hell and back.

"I owe you an apology for being so rude this morning. I didn't mean to imply anything bad," she stammered.

He waved his hand at her to just forget it. "You were talking about spirits and ghosts. Do you believe in the supernatural?"

"Not really," she said.

He moved his face closer so they were nose to nose. Peppermint mingled with his breath. "Maybe, there is a ghost between us. Your brother has thrown us together. Do you really think it is a coincidence that out of all the thousands mourning at Ground Zero, it happened to be me you bumped into?" he said.

His eyes never wavered from hers, and it felt like a spider danced on her back. *Two kindred souls will meet, no matter how far they have to come, if they are destined to be together. Nonsense!* She laughed uncomfortably and changed the subject. "You said they don't often let you out of your cubicle. Are you imprisoned at a zoo?"

"It was a poor attempt at a joke," he said, running his finger around the collar of his shirt as though the material pricked him. There was an ugly gash across his neck that looked like a rope burn.

"Tell me about Jake," she said with a touch of pleading in her voice. "We were torn apart after our parents' deaths and sent to different foster homes, where we weren't allowed to communicate. The powers that be felt we would adjust, if we forgot one another."

A curtain folded across his face. He hummed, tapping his boot against the sidewalk. "I should be getting back," he said, as if they spent the afternoon together instead of just minutes, as if his time was too valuable to waste on her.

With a reddened face she looked at her watch. The lunch hour was about over. "I'm sorry. I didn't mean to keep you from your work."

"It's not that." Once again, he clutched that battered wallet so tightly, his hand reddened.

She stroked his arm. "Please," she said, squeezing his biceps. Her voice lowered, cracking like ice. "All these years, I've wondered about my brother. I tried so hard to find him. I thought I never would, and now this," she said, waving her arm at the bent steel on Cortlandt Street. Parts of the Twin Towers looked like metal spaghetti.

He sighed and slapped the wallet back in his pocket. He shifted his eyes to the wreckage of the South Tower. "I was just settling down for another boring day at the office, when the plane hit," he mumbled.

"Please tell me what happened to Jake," she said, tugging on his arm.

"The reason I'm here is to do whatever is in my power to help your brother. I owe him," he said.

"Owe him for what?"

He wiped his mouth with a shaky finger, like he needed another stiff drink. "Your brother is a damned good man."

"Is a good man? Haven't you heard? The rescue operation is now a recovery operation," she said bitterly.

"Come on," he ordered in a gruff voice.

Miranda hesitated, thinking she was a woman all alone in the big bad city, known for its crime. Never talk to strangers, she was taught as a girl but with a child's curiosity, there were a lot of questions about Jake, even though she feared the answers.

So, Miranda followed the stranger named Christopher Michaels.

§

Chapter 7:1

And life will grow from the ashes.

They kept walking, she silently behind.

Ashes ran on his short legs, trying to keep up. Miranda had discovered that Ashes didn't need the leash she bought. The dog obediently followed her, or stayed where he was told to.

Ashes was a smart little dog. He knew when to hide.

Michaels seemed to have forgotten her.

Maybe he's going back to work, if he has a new workplace to go to that is.

He stopped and she bumped into him.

Michaels had led her to Battery Park at the southern tip of Manhattan. The park was less than a mile from the Twin Tower ruins and was eerily cloaked in dusty cobwebs and ash a foot deep.

"When the towers fell, 125 tons of ash landed on Battery Park. When it comes to dying, there's not a lot of difference between a man and a plant," he said, shrugging his broad shoulders.

Yet, there were a few flowers growing from the ashes.

Battery Park wasn't the largest park in the city, but it boasted the best benches for gazing out to sea. There were plenty of empty benches, all covered with such thick dust, it could only be from a good majority of the Twin Towers disintegrating into dust when the buildings pancaked and some of the ash scattering to Battery Park.

Michaels veered to the left and walked over to a park bench, patting the seat beside him. Dust from the bench swirled about his hand. He smiled like a cold shark, making her wonder about her sanity when she cleaned off the seat. She plopped down alongside him, nudging her hip into the opposite corner.

"This is my bench. My initials are carved into the seat. Right there. Under your pretty ass," he said.

She read the initials CBM carved into the wood of the bench. "Christopher B. Michaels. What's the B for? Bastard?"

"Brian," he said, laughing. "Now why are you looking at me like that? Because I used the word, ass or because I said your ass was pretty?"

"I thought only the homeless carved their names into park benches," she snapped.

"And you think that I'm a damn drunk and homeless?"

Miranda shrugged her shoulders. *If the shoe fits, as the saying goes,* she thought, wrinkling her nose at his bloodshot eyes and stained pants. The crease was crisp, but…

"Woodworkers like to carve their names on their possessions," he said, leaning against the bench and stretching out his long legs.

"And egomaniacs," she added, focusing on the sea that was less disturbing than this man, who crawled under her skin, bringing out the worst in her.

A dusty squirrel scampered down a tree, stood on its hind legs, and wiggled its whiskers nibbling on a nut. She smiled and looked at Michaels, but he wasn't interested in the squirrel. He was staring at her legs.

I shouldn't have worn such a short dress, she thought, crossing her boots. She folded her hands across her thighs, clasping her fingers so her skin whitened.

He relaxed against the bench, crossing his ankle over his thigh. He wiggled his scuffed shoe that was covered in ash from Ground Zero. "So you want to know about Jacob, the man."

She plunked her purse between them. "I want to know everything. Did you know Jake long?"

"The Asters bloomed early this year," he said, nodding at drooping flowers covered with dusty lace. "Life is all in the timing, isn't it? One can't fight fate."

"Look," she said, pointing to a lone, purple, daisy-like flower bursting through the ashes.

He stared at her instead, in a way that made her pulse race.

"And what of you, Mandy? Are you strong like that flower?"

"What do you mean?" She looked down at the bench and away from his disturbing eyes.

"I mean, can you bear to hear what I have to tell you? Can you survive the devastation of 9/11?"

She wrote 9/11 on the dusty bench. The Statue of Liberty was visible in the distance. "I imagine that gift over there from the people of France, our grand Lady in Green, cries for her children. Plaster of Paris tears stream down her face as she points her eternal flame of freedom towards the heavens. Ground Zero is a fitting name for the aftermath of September 11th. The big hole left by the Twin Towers looks like a big zero next to the skyscrapers hovering around it."

"When it comes to dying, there's not a lot of difference between a man and a skyscraper," he said.

"There were many accounts of people who survived the attacks," she said.

"But you haven't heard the tale of someone who died," he said, pinching her chin and forcing her to look at him.

He was the most frustrating man, ever. His judging eyes made her feel guilty for just being alive. She had no choice but to hang out with him for now. He held the key to opening the doors to Jake's life. Maybe, he could even unlock the mystery of his death so she might lay her brother to rest. He hinted at such knowledge. Miranda took a deep breath, swallowing the foul park air.

Michaels casually stretched a long arm across the bench. He lifted her hair, draping it across his arm. Fine hairs from his hand brushed against her neck, causing goose bumps to blister her skin. She sat stiffly, her back propped against the wooden slats of the bench. Miranda wished he had not broken her sunglasses. He never apologized. She suspected Michaels stomped on the lenses on purpose so she couldn't hide from him.

Stupid idea, that. Now why would he even care?

His jugular vein beat against his shaven skin. His masculine throat was tanned and healthy looking. Chest hairs peeked out at the base of his throat. She insanely wanted to move closer and rub against his skin like a cat. Miranda swallowed, digging her nails into her palms

He twitched his lips, and she could tell by his eyes he was aware of her attraction to him, even stained and beaten-looking as he was.

She self-consciously cupped her cheek, covering her ugly-looking, knife scar.

Their breathing was synchronized, their heartbeats timed together. His damned fingers touched the back of her neck, barely, not enough to mean anything, and just enough to make her shiver. Michaels had the sort of manly voice that rocks a woman's stomach and makes her yearn for…

I damn well better get myself under control!

Miranda swore he could read minds and sensed the danger she was in, even as he began to speak about her brother.

§

Chapter 8:1

And the roar of ships will be heard
Traveling across the vast ocean
Towards the dark,
Even as the roar of feet will be heard
Traveling across the bridge
Towards the light.

"Jacob Balboa," Michaels softly said and clutched his hands, his knuckles whitening. He took a flask of liquor from his pocket and sipped.

"I used to eat lunch sitting on this bench and stare out to sea, wishing I was anywhere but here. Now, this is the only place I want to be." He inhaled deeply, filling his lungs with park stench.

Yuck! Battery Park smelled like stale water in a jar of cut flowers that hadn't been changed in weeks.

"And where do you live? Texas?" he said with a catch to his voice that claimed his city could kick her city's ass, no matter what city she lived in.

Jake must have told him about Texas, her home until she graduated from high school. Perhaps, her brother's ghost sat between them. She rubbed the wooden bench, holding her breath, listening for the slightest sound, and waiting for the lightest touch. A ray of sunlight warmed her face—Jake, his ghost.

Michaels cleared his throat. "I didn't ask for your exact address, merely the general location. The question is a no brainer."

"I live in Los Angeles but keep a P.O. Box in Austin with a forwarding address just in case."

"Your brother ever tried to find you. Save you some money and cancel the box because he's dead," Michaels said.

He didn't have to be so cruel nor look so angry.

"I never minded the money," she said in a small voice.

"Well, money was once everything to me before. Now I'm broke on my ass and don't give a shit!"

They sat in silence while he stared out to sea with a dark look. Michaels had not wanted to be with her. He tried to escape her at Ground Zero, but she begged and pleaded with him to tell her about Jake.

"So why the heck did you ever leave Texas?" he grunted as if the words were forced from his throat. His interest in her seemed to go against his better judgment and his will.

"I never wanted to get out of any place as bad as I did Austin," she said with a frankness that surprised her. Michaels was able to draw her out of herself. He would make a good detective.

Indeed. He leaned towards her like an interrogator. "So why did you move from Austin, your hometown?"

She shrugged her shoulders. "I don't know. Nothing good ever happened to me there. Austin was just an unhappy place for me to be so, when I was released from the detention…, uh received a scholarship from the University of California, I ran. I figured if I moved, I would be happy."

"And are you?"

"Not on a personal level."

"That's too bad," he said.

She hated sympathy. "Poor, poor Miranda," the Social Services caseworker always said when she sent her to live with yet another family. "Miranda Balboa, you are a horror. You're lucky I found a new family to take you in. You're getting a reputation, young as you are. Poor Miranda." She had hated poor, pathetic Miranda whom nobody wanted around.

She told Michaels, "I think total happiness is unattainable. Either people are happy with their job, finances, family, religion or love. I don't believe anyone is happy with everything."

"That's a cynical attitude for one so young. How many have you struck out on?"

"Three out of five, still forty percent isn't bad. It is not a perfect world."

"Which three have you struck out on?"

"Family, religion and love," she said, bristling at the pity in his eyes. "What about you? Are you ever happy?"

"I used to be. Had it all, four out of four," he said with a cockiness grating on her nerves.

"Just four out of four? What happened to the fifth?"

"There is no such thing as romantic love to make the world go around. Never has been. Never will be," he said, snorting.

"What does make the world go around then?" she said, *smart ass.*

"I used to think money spun the world on its axis."

"You used to?"

"Let's just say since 9/11 I've had a change of heart. However, I still believe women prefer the security of money to so-called love."

"Emotional noninvolvement is safer. Always has been. Always will be," she said flatly.

"Good. We agree then not to fall in love."

"Well, I don't like moody men," she scoffed. "Shouldn't you call your office and tell them you got sick at lunch or something?"

"No one will miss me." His eyes sparkled with amusement. He rose to his feet and stretched. "Come on," he said, offering her his hand.

She was normally not vain, but did not want Michaels to see her knife scar, which she still hid behind her hand. Miranda hesitated before placing her other hand in his.

He yanked her to her feet like he was pulling teeth. "I guess you're looking for the perfect man to sweep you off your feet," he said, laughing.

"A perfect man? Shoot, that's a new one."

"Are you waiting for a knight in shining armor, Mandy?" he said in a voice making fun of her.

"Fairy tales," she snorted, flinching at her nickname. She hated him calling her Mandy. She did not even like the man.

"I think I'm beginning to like you, Mandy. Take that guarded look off your face. You're not my type. You're too skinny, but you have strength and intelligence. You're not the dewy-eyed, man-crazy, chasing-after-anything-in-a-pair-of-pants cunt just to get-that-ring-on-her-finger type."

"You can let my hand go now, and thanks for the compliment," she coldly said.

He cursed, releasing her so she almost fell over backward.

He swaggered down the walkway with the manners of a New Yorker. Surviving in the concrete jungle makes sarcasm second nature. He had a haughty voice New Yorkers are so good at. Manhattan was a city that sold t-shirts with the slogan, *My City Can Kick Your City's Ass.*

Fuming, she followed. They had not spoken much about Jake. No telling where Michaels was headed.

"Seaport," he answered as if he heard her thoughts. "You've got to be hungry. They have great shrimp cocktails with shrimp the size of…." He held up a fist and punched the air in a macho, childish way.

"Your bench isn't the most comfortable," she yelled.

"I know. My initials on the bench are embedded on your ass."

She glared at his back and shook her legs, trying to restore the blood flow.

His golden head shone like a beacon in a city where he was her lifeline, besides the dog prancing beside her with his tail stiff in the air. "I think he's forgotten about us," she said, scooping Ashes in her arms and jerking her head sideways to avoid his tongue and doggy breath.

They headed toward the East River. The fishy air was refreshing compared to Ground Zero air, which included Battery Park. The ocean air opened her lungs, making her chest hurt.

Michaels seemed to have forgotten about her as he took in the sites of the centuries old Seaport with hungry eyes, as if seeing it for the very first time.

It's not normally this deserted, she thought, her heels echoing on the cobblestone walkway. Crowds normally lingered in front of the two-story Fulton Market. A scattering of people strolled about. It was a bit chilly for any of the outdoor cafes at Cannon's Walk housing a block of buildings from the last two centuries. Very few were out shopping.

Warships manned the harbor, protecting Lady Liberty who stood between the modern warships and centuries old sailing ships docked at Seaport. The boats' sails were at half-mast. A paddle wheel boat normally cruised the Hudson with gawky tourists and locals hanging over its railings. The boat now spun its paddle wheels in the dock—going nowhere.

Battleships bobbed on the horizon, projecting an uneasy feeling.

Michaels paid no attention to the modern ships of war but stared, like in a trance, at historic sailing ships lined up in homage to a bygone era.

"If it was dawn, we would be watching men unload fish from refrigerated trucks. The Fulton Fish market isn't what it used to be though," he lamented. "They once sold fresh fish straight from the boats. Can you imagine that? I would have loved to have been a merchant seaman on a sailing ship 125 years ago with the wind in my hair and the taste of the sea in my mouth. The vastness of the ocean gives one a sense of freedom."

Michaels was a romantic—he just didn't know it.

"Did Jake ever sail," she said.

"I wish, but hardly ever had the time. Too busy trying to get rich. But it would have been something, to see the port the way it was in its heyday as a major port, instead of touristy," he said, confusing her. Why didn't he answer her questions about Jake? What a self-centered asshole!

"Come on. Let's go feed you," he said.

Pier 17 announced its presence on Seaport in big white letters on a red wall. The pier was three stories of shopping and eating. They stood on the top floor. Ashes stared up at Michaels with an expectant look on the dog's face.

Michaels played with his food, looking longingly at sailing ships harbored on the East River.

She ate a gigantic shrimp cocktail and eyed the bridge, connecting Manhattan to Brooklyn some three miles away. Today was like any normal day and a congestion of cars, buses, and taxicabs traveled across the Brooklyn Bridge, an engineering marvel, considering it was built in 1883. The morning of 9/11, only human traffic stampeded across the bridge, refugees running from the WTC terror.

When the towers burst into flames, black smoke engulfed the city, afflicting Manhattan with darkness. The combined stories of both buildings, all 220 floors, fell gracefully in the path of least destruction, straight down, as if a special-effects wizard set up the scene for a one-time camera shot.

Miranda closed her eyes, remembering the look of horror on people's faces as they ran from the collapsing buildings. Their panic was shown live on television.

Michaels threw down his napkin and stomped away from the table without a word. He stood at the railing, his fingers clinging to the pipe. He had the look of a man wanting to jump. Michaels probably had Post Traumatic Stress Syndrome, or survivor's guilt, or maybe he carried other baggage, and 9/11 was just another suitcase.

She longed to ask Michaels if he had been one of those refugees on the Brooklyn Bridge that day.

He pointed out the Statue of Liberty. "The inscription at the bottom of the statue reads, Give me your tired, your poor, and your huddled masses yearning to breathe free. The wretched refuse of your teeming shore. And your totally fucked up core," he said.

She and Michaels had something in common, besides Jake—they both were damaged goods.

Miranda wanted to ask Michaels about Jake but he looked so pissed off. You can follow a man to water, but you can't force him to drink—Michaels had no problem drinking on his own. You can follow a man to his past, but you can't force him to talk about it.

Women have been following men since the dawn of time.

Michaels did not go back to their table. Miranda was stuck with the check, paying for both their meals. She supposed it was the price she had to pay for information about her brother.

Miranda threw her plastic utensils in the trash and followed Michaels, wondering where he was leading her, and when the heck he was going to talk about her brother.

§

Chapter 9:1

On Wall Street there is a bull
With the meanest eyes ever cast in bronze
Ready to gore the terrorists.

One can never really experience Manhattan except in person, not even on an IMAX screen. All the skyscrapers of San Francisco and Houston could be dropped into the southern tip of Manhattan, and still skyscrapers would fan northward for well over 100 blocks, filling up the gap between the Hudson and East Rivers. Since 9/11 happened, the skyscrapers appeared to be leaning towards one another. If architecture could speak like paintings do, the buildings would bemoan their fragility.

Michaels led Miranda to Wall Street. The New York Stock Exchange was and the Twin Towers had been in the financial district. Stock brokers walked around with surgical masks on their long faces, appearing like hypochondriacs.

"You should get a mask to protect you from the poisoned air coming from Ground Zero," Michaels said.

"So should you."

He simply shrugged his shoulders.

Near Wall Street and Broadway was a landmark plaque stating it was named Wall Street because a wall once protected the city from attack by enemies and warring Indians.

"Manhattan should rebuild the wall for which Wall Street was named," she said.

"It would have to be a hell of a high wall," he said, insisting she buy herself a mask.

She bought a bag of surgery-like masks.

He ripped open the bag, placing a mask over her nose and mouth.

She handed him a mask.

He turned white, appearing panic stricken. "I wouldn't be able to breathe with that thing. Claustrophobic," he said.

There was a life-size, bronze bull poised to charge on Wall Street. Michaels patted the bull's rump and said, "Your brother was a geek toiling in a sweatshop startup, blinded by the deceptive shine of gold. Where do you work, Mandy? You a reporter? Palm reader? Gypsy? Tease? A shrink?"

Standing in the hub of the world's financial markets, big money, wheeling and dealing, fame, fortune, even the throbbing agony of misfortune, made her life seem unexciting. She felt loathe to confess that, "Actually I'm an elementary school teacher. I shape eight-year-old minds and in return, the children unlock their hearts and let me in."

Miranda braced herself for a subtle put-down because he was a hot shot New Yorker. Instead, he surprised her. "Teaching children is a commendable profession," he said, looking sincerely like he meant it. "So do you also teach Sunday School?"

Ah, the poisonous icing on the cake. His tone of voice mocked her like she was Saint Miranda. If he only knew the truth about her wild youth, how she sold pot in high school, ran out of restaurants without paying, and shoplifted until she was caught too many times and locked up at a juvenile detention facility until the age of eighteen.

"I never go to church," she said, rubbing the scar on her face.

"You told me you struck out on religion. You've really given up on God?"

"How can you believe in God after 9/11? You, of all people! You were at the World Trade Center on that day."

"On the contrary, when you see people killed yet others survive the same odds, it makes you realize there is a God. 9/11 could have been a lot worse. The Towers could have fallen across in a domino effect and not straight down."

"I did believe in God, once, but I've let Him down too many times," she softly said.

"You mean, you think He's given up on you. Don't let unhappiness make you bitter against God. Man makes his own destiny. Happiness comes from in here," he said, touching a finger to her head. "Peace comes from within." He placed a hand over her heart.

"You and I aren't so very different, Michaels. You may not be a romantic but you are religious. There are similarities."

"Bullshit! The only similarity between being religious and romantic is both require faith. This is all superficial crap," he said, sweeping his arm at Wall Street. "God and family are what really matters. People, not money."

"One doesn't realize how important family is until one is alone," she said.

"Yes," he agreed, still holding his hand over her heart. "I don't want to hurt you, Mandy."

"Then don't. Just tell me the truth about Jake. How can you hurt me? What is it you're keeping from me?"

Michaels grabbed onto her jacket, and then lowered his trembling hand. He took a step back, shoving his hands in his pockets. He looked down at the sidewalk and swallowed. "I'm up to my neck now. Let's just say, I've developed a soft spot for you. You look so damned helpless in my city. Bullshit! I am not going to play the knight-in-shining-armor crap!"

"Nobody asked you to, and your armor is exceedingly dull. I am not helpless. I have made my own way longer than you have. Give me something about Jake. Anything! You talked about this and that?"

"Yeah," he grunted like she wrung the word from him.

"You spoke about each other's families?"

"At times," he said, guardedly.

"Did Jake ever speak about me?"

He stared silently back at her.

"Never?" she said.

"I wish I could lie to you, Mandy but Jake only mentioned you once."

She flinched like he struck her.

"I can imagine what it must be like to lose your family," he said, looking heartbroken, the faker.

"No, you can't. You have no idea," she said, feeling like pounding his chest and screaming. She hadn't felt this way since she was a teen and regularly threw fits about anything and everything. It took a lot of talks in the mirror, self-berating and self-encouragement to outgrow her childishness, but she learned to control her emotions.

He reached out a hand to her and then shoved his hands back in his pockets. He had the saddest look on his face, and she reached out to him. Just a touch on his arm.

He must be lonely; she thought with disbelief that a man as beautiful as him would be alone. Miranda never before this moment experienced the melding of her heart, mind and soul with another so strongly. When he breathed, she breathed. Their hearts beat in unison. Their chests rose and fell together. *This must be what soul mates are all about,* she thought, wishing she could read his mind instead of just feeling his emotions, without really understanding why he seemed to be alienated.

Don't be stupid! For all you know, he may be married. Brace yourself and expect him to say—I'm lonely. My wife doesn't understand me.

Idiot! Don't get involved with his problems. And he is not your soul mate.

She took a step back from him.

"I think it's going to rain," he said, scanning the sky. "I love the feel of water on my face, that damp fresh smell carrying away the stink."

Just like that he switched from looking like a tortured soul to being in love with the rain.

Miranda could care less about the rain or if she got soaked. "Do you know how Jake died?" she said, choking back her tears.

Michaels stared off into the distance and clenched his jaw. He turned and walked away.

She reached out her hand to his back then rubbed her forehead. *Dummy, now look what you've done. Gone and scared him off with your tears.* Michaels left her standing between two columns which held up the public entrance of the New York Stock Exchange.

What really ate at her, what Miranda really searched for was the answer to the question nagging her ever since Jake's face flashed across her television screen—was this Jacob Balboa in the printout really Jake? Her Jake?

She looked at her brother's poster, wistfully thinking, *he doesn't look so much like Jake after all*, but the face in the poster was exactly like she remembered their father. She tried to picture the young Jake. He had rarely smiled. Instead he laughed, opening his mouth wide and showing off the many fillings Miranda was jealous of when they were little.

She dropped Jake's picture and the paper floated like a feather to her feet. She gawked at three glass doors at the entrance to the Stock Exchange. A man's reflection stared back at her from the middle glass door. He was tall and thin, dressed in jeans and a techie t-shirt proclaiming the name of a startup. She could make out the words EGGHEAD in big red letters across his t-shirt.

Frozen, she stared back at her brother, the same ghost who appeared to her at Ground Zero and then in her dream last night. He was the same man in the printout at her feet. He must be her Jake else, *why would his ghost seek me out? The missing Jacob Balboa would not haunt me, unless there is a connection between us, a bond stronger than death.*

§

Chapter 10:1

And cynicism will reign.

Jake's reflection twisted and misshaped, as though he couldn't quite make the transition between the world of the living and the spirit world. His reflection waffled within the glass door.

"Jake. Oh Jake," she whispered.

For the life of her Miranda couldn't move her feet closer to the door and help him. Maybe if she concentrated her will, she could touch him. *Jake. Jake. Jake,* she thought.

He opened his mouth and screamed at her but she couldn't hear what he said. He wiggled, pounding his fists. He was trapped inside the glass.

Fading. Appearing. Fading. Appearing.

"Mandy," a soft voice spoke behind her.

She jumped, expecting Jake to be standing at her back.

It was Michaels.

"He's gone," Miranda said in a tiny voice as she peered at the people going in and out of the glass doors of the Stock Exchange. She shivered and hugged her arms.

"No, I'm right here," Michaels said, balancing a cup of hot chocolate in his hands. "Drink this. It will warm you."

"You scared him off."

He simply shook his head and looked at her like she was crazy.

You saw him didn't you, Ashes?

The dog looked straight ahead as if in a trance.

Poor dog must be suffering from post traumatic stress, too. I've never seen a stranger animal in my whole life.

She felt like crying again when Michaels snapped an umbrella open, holding it over her. *Why does he suddenly have to be so kind?*

Miranda held the cup of hot cocoa with trembling hands and raised it to her lips. She sipped the drink, spilling drops of the beverage. *Get a grip, Miranda, you're losing it.*

"Are you okay?" he said.

"Mm," she said, nodding her head and swallowing the cocoa. She forced herself to concentrate on the hot liquid scorching her throat. She wouldn't mention ghosts to him again. Once was bad enough. Twice, and he would think her insane.

"Where did you get the umbrella?" she said.

"From the man on the corner. I took it when he wasn't looking," he said, raising his eyebrows at her exasperated look. He looked pleased with himself that he carried off the theft without being noticed. "It was too easy," he said, laughing.

"I used to shoplift when I was a kid," she blurted out, appalled that she confessed such a thing to him. She never told a living soul before and even lied when caught red-handed.

"Did you get caught?" he said.

"How did you know I like marshmallows?" she said, changing the subject from her criminal past.

"You look like a marshmallow girl."

"Soft and easily burned?" she said with dismay.

"On the outside, Mandy, you may be soft, but you must be a strong woman due to your hard childhood."

"You have no idea what I'm like," she said in an unsteady voice.

"I bet you'd be a formidable opponent."

"I'm not sure I could fight you."

He cocked his head, a sparkle lighting his eyes.

She blew on the hot cup of chocolate. *I should just get it over with and burn my tongue off.*

He ran a finger down her cheek. His callus scraping against her skin made her weak at the knees. *This man is a hard New Yorker while I'm really too soft. How about mushy?*

"You look tired. I should be going," he said.

She forgot to ask him when and if she'd see him again. Michaels must have turned a corner somewhere. He simply vanished in the crowd.

She looked for him, up and down Wall Street, and around Broad Street. The area was a concrete maze, dwarfed by skyscrapers. It was only four o'clock but the sun had ducked behind the buildings in a typical Manhattan sunset. Elongated shadows of men dressed in business suits and hats crawled up the walls of the buildings, down the streets and across the sidewalks.

She shoved her hand into her pocket and pulled out the rumpled napkin where he had scribbled his number. The words, *cell phone*, were in bold black letters on the napkin, but the numbers below were faded. Funny, the cell number on the napkin had been written in ink as dark as the words, *cell phone*, above his now faded phone number. Disappearing ink, just like him. Miranda blew her nose with the napkin that smelled like ashes—welcome to New York City.

"Did you see where he went?" she asked Ashes. "Michaels was standing on the corner. He had four directions to choose. He could have ducked into any of the buildings and a few unsavory alleys."

Ashes lowered his head and whined as if sworn to secrecy.

"Some bloodhound you make. Come on. We better head back to the Algonquin."

She eyed the subway station entrance, but September 11th and the threat of terrorists was too recent. "I am tired. We'll splurge and catch a cab."

Miranda stepped off the curb and onto Broadway. She held a hand up to a yellow taxi like she had seen New Yorkers do.

A couple of cabs whizzed by. Michaels was right. She was helpless in his city. "Shithead," she muttered to a back bumper. She resisted the urge to flip off the cabbie. He had an unsavory look like the rest of Manhattan at dusk, before the city lit up like candles on a 100-foot wedding cake.

After being rejected by three more cabs, a passerby explained to her to look for a cab with the numbers on the roof lit up and the words *off duty* unlit.

She now felt foolish cussing at the cabs that sped by without stopping.

At least it was no longer raining. Miranda snapped the umbrella shut, buttoned her jacket and hoofed it, splashing her shoes against the sidewalk. She hunted for a cab. Finally, she got lucky and was picked up on Broadway and St. John.

The cab sped away.

Bobbing in the crowd on Fulton Street was a familiar face.

"Turn right and follow that blonde man," Miranda yelled at the driver.

He screeched the tires around the corner and stepped on the gas. "What blonde man, miss?"

"Michaels…he was just here. I…I could have sworn," she mumbled.

"Where to? Ground Zero?"

"Drive around a bit and maybe we'll find him," she said.

Miranda twisted her head in all directions, looking for Michaels.

But like before, he was nowhere to be found.

§

Chapter 11:1

In dreams they will come.

The Algonquin Hotel

Over the years, she spoke to her brother in her head and out loud in empty rooms. The conversations were all one-way. Through all the passing years, it was the phantom Jake who knew her hopes, dreams, fears, and schemes, most of which went astray.

That's right, Jake. I haven't changed much. I'm still the total screw up, except with the children. At least, I got one thing right. My life hasn't been a total waste, she thought, tossing her wet tissue into a trash can.

All she managed to get out of Michaels was that Jake only spoke about her once. "Just once," she told Ashes. "At least my brother didn't forget about me completely."

By the look on his face when she asked Michaels how Jake died, she suspected he might know.

Miranda flipped through the Manhattan phone book of personal listings, doctor listings, therapists and counselors, but there was no Michaels listed. She then called information for Queens, Brooklyn, Staten Island, Long Island, the Bronx, and Hoboken. Again, there was no listing for any Michaels. She even tried Newark. She had no way to get in touch with him.

She threw the phone book at the wall. *He should have told me more about Jake.*

She ordered room service and ate a leisurely supper tasting like sawdust.

Miranda readied for bed and flipped through a magazine, not really reading the words.

The pictures in the magazine grew fuzzy and she fell asleep.

A dream transported her to *Battery Park and a gray, garden world of drooping flowers.*

Leafless trees cast spindly shadows upon the dusty ground.

She was alone, yet could not shake the feeling that—someone's watching me.

She inched closer to the corner of Michael's bench.

The branches of the trees rubbed against each other, screeching like violins.

Shadows of branches, resembling skeletal fingers, crept towards her.

What was that noise?

She moved closer to the bench arm—not that the bench will protect me.

Over there. Behind a tree.

Eyes peered at her.

She could have sworn she saw something, someone move in the shadows. She could have sworn.

Hands massaged her shoulders.

She slapped at her neck, but nothing was there.

Hot breath blew at the crown of her hair, followed by a deep sigh.

She yelped and jumped from the bench.

Miranda scurried north along the Hudson River.

A pirate ship with cobwebs for sails bobbed in the harbor, the lone ship in the sea. A black flag with a skull waved from its bow.

A tsunami rushed from Ellis Island.

Miranda held her breath, expecting the gigantic wave to sweep her away to New Jersey.

A huge Statue of Liberty rose from behind the ship, a green lady with shoulders slouched and torch lowered. The tsunami splashed against the lady's back, which protected the city from drowning.

Puffs of fog smelling like breath mints blew across her shoulder.

Footsteps pounded behind her.

She mewed, expanding her lungs and running faster.

Miranda darted towards Winter Garden—the glass-domed man-made wonder stretching 120 feet high.

Ah, no. The Winter Garden was mortally wounded from behind when the Twin Towers collapsed.

Miranda coughed and yanked a surgical mask over her mouth and nose.

She pulled open a door, tiptoeing through broken glass.

On her right was a beauty shop with an empty chair, eerily spinning. A nauseous stink of permanents and hair dye drifted out the door, mixing with the smell of freshly-brewed espresso and chocolate-covered strawberries.

At a watch store all the clocks were stopped at 10:28, the time the North Tower collapsed.

The vaulted glass roof of the atrium was damaged with missing and broken panes.

The green steel frames were gray with ashes.

Dust on the marble floor swept across her ankles, broken tiles moving beneath her.

A forest of trees stretched from beneath the floor, dusting the glass ceiling with palms. The palms were dying from glass cuts or already dead, choking on poisonous fumes. Soot covered the benches surrounding the trees.

In the glass wall behind the trees was a jagged hole, looking as if a huge puzzle piece was missing.

At the east end of the atrium was a mangled mess of garbage piled about six stories high.

There was a noise at the entrance, and footsteps walking across the floor. Dust clouds swirled, forming the shape of a man.

When the dust cleared, Miranda stared into Michaels' savage eyes.

She shook her head no and ran towards the grand staircase, half of which was still standing, the other half fallen by tons of debris. The staircase once led to a bridge connecting to the North Tower. The bridge had toppled with the towers.

Miranda shifted her eyes to the glass roof of the atrium. Steel beams were broken and glass panes missing. There was a hole in the sky where the Twin Towers had been.

A haunting tune came from below. At the broken glass wall, Jake played the piano. He was covered in ash, except for a white orchid in his lapel.

He wore black tails and a bow tie covered with cobwebs. Behind him, where the glass was broken, the sun shone brightly off the Hudson River, lighting him up like the Phantom of the Opera.

His fingers traveled across the keys, playing Somewhere Over the Rainbow. *Lighted wreaths hung from broken steel beams, fading in and out with each tingling key.*

"Jake, I'm over here," she yelled.

He crooned a rowdy song, off-key. "One-hundred bottles of beer on the wall."

She could see right through him to the Hudson River.

Michaels charged towards the grand staircase.

Many of the steps were cracked and lined with mud. Chunks were missing from the railing. How foolish to climb a broken staircase, but Jake's ghost doesn't scare me. I'm terrified of Michaels.

Oh, God, here he comes!

Michaels chased her up the stairs, tripping and nearly falling on broken marble.

His legs were longer and he was taking the stairs two at a time.

He reached out an arm, grabbed her around the waist, and lifted her in the air.

Miranda dangled at the top of the wobbling staircase.

He pulled her towards him, crushing her to his chest.

"Mandy, don't be afraid. Trust me. Let me," he whispered, kissing her neck. Then he yanked the mask from her face.

The air is toxic. I can't breathe; she thought and punched his shoulder.

He twisted her wrists behind her back, pulling her down on the step. The staircase shook, its hinges grinding and loosening.

She gulped, looking over the ragged edge to the carnage below.

He gripped her face, slamming his lips on hers.

Moaning, she kissed him back.

He covered her with his body, shielding her from falling glass.

There was a grinding noise.

The braces broke.

The staircase went whirling towards the floor, hitting the marble with a crash.

Miranda awoke, gasping and sweating, with her head hanging over the mattress.

Someone lay on top of her, slobbering kisses on her face.

"Michaels?" she said, groggily.

Doggy breath.

"Ashes," she groaned.

The dog wagged his tail against her stomach, yapping.

Miranda groaned and kicked herself. She only met the man yesterday, and here she was dreaming of Michaels lying on top of her, kissing her.

Miranda cussed at herself for not forcing him to tell her about Jake.

§

Chapter 12:1

And their names shall number in the thousands.

Saturday, September 22, 2001

Miranda woke up in a foul mood from lack of sleep and dreaming about Michaels. In all probability, she would never see him again.

Who was there to find out what happened to Jake but her? She was his only family. Well, perhaps not. He might have fallen in love, married, and had children. Jake may not have been emotionally constipated and damaged like she was.

Miranda scanned the telephone book for Jake's address again, in case she missed it. There was no Jacob Balboa listed in the New York City phone book. She dialed information and learned there was a J. Balboa with an unlisted number. The operator refused to give out the number, even to a sister looking for her long-lost brother.

After many phone calls she dialed a number for Egghead Revolution. The company had two offices, one in Manhattan and another in San Jose, California. "Jacob's records show he had no family. If you want to collect on the company life insurance, you'll have to get a lawyer," an official told her.

"I just want his address," she said.

"We can't give out his address. Looters. His landlord will have to deal with it."

"Who is his landlord?"

"I can't tell you that. Sorry."

Click.

"Asshole," she screamed into the phone.

Miranda slammed the phone down. She yanked the phone from the socket, throwing it against the wall. She did not want a lawyer or to file for Jake's life insurance money. She didn't even care to know how much. She just wanted to get to know him through his stuff in his apartment.

Ashes stared at her with a concerned look in his big eyes.

"You know what it's like don't you, Ashes? You've lost your family, too, and no one has called about your advertisement. Well, I tried to claim Jake, but it's hard to prove I'm his sister when he listed himself as having no family. He forgot about me, unless the Jacob Balboa from Egghead Revolution is not my brother," she said, frowning.

More confused than ever, she pulled out the wrinkled missing poster. Jake or Jacob looked so alive in the picture. His eyes sparkled with a remembered mischief. It was not surprising he dressed like a geek with a t-shirt blaring out his startup's name and the words 'We Rule'. Jake was always good at math and loved computer games. It was quite probable her brother would have worked for Egghead Revolution.

Come on, Mandy, play Nintendo with me, he would pester her when they were kids.

But, Jake, you're too good.

Let's play Mario Brothers. I'll give you a handicap.

Jake did more than that. He was smarter, his reflexes faster, yet he lost on purpose and laughed when she squealed with excitement.

She had not felt this close to him since they were separated. Just being in the same city Jake lived in was heartwarming, even given the depressive air of 9/11. Miranda wished she knew where his apartment was located. She didn't have to go into the building even, just sit outside and imagine that she didn't need Michaels.

§§§

Miranda was still in a melancholy mood when a cab left her at Ground Zero. Today was a special ceremony of the reading of the names of all who perished.

A man next to her cuffed his ears with his hands. He stared at the rubble of Ground Zero with such intensity.

A spirit is here for him, too.

"Cold. You're so cold," he said, stretching out his arms as though he touched a ghost's palms.

The man paid no heed when the reading of the victims' names began. He talked to himself, ignoring the pleas around him for silence.

"Hush."

"Sh."

"Be quiet."

"Shut up."

"Kook."

Miranda had difficulty concentrating on the names called out because she scanned Ground Zero for a tall man with golden hair. Occasionally she would spot a likely suspect, only to be let down because he wasn't her Michaels.

Don't you dare think that! Ever! He's not your Michaels.

Half an hour passed with one name following the next in alphabetical order. She forced herself to concentrate on the names being announced over the microphone. She mumbled each victim's name to show her respect, struggling to stay awake, and her head wobbling on her shoulders.

I've got to stay awake. I don't want to miss Jake's name.

Her eyelids grew heavy. She leaned against a wall, nodding off to sleep.

A voice whispered in her ear, "Wake up, Sleepy Head."

She rubbed her eyes, yawning.

"You look like a little girl all rumpled from sleep."

"It's you," she squeaked.

"In the flesh," Michaels said.

"But I thought..."

"Oh yeah?"

She blushed.

"I figured I'd find you at the reading of the names," he said.

"But there are so many people here and yet you found me. How…"

"I've been searching for you for a long time." Michaels touched his fingers to her lips and pointed his chin at the man announcing the names.

"Jacob Balboa," was called out.

Jake's death was now final, but Miranda felt no closure. It was like a lion clawed her chest.

Michaels pulled her into his arms, patting her head and rumpling her hair with his large hand. "Sh. It's all right. Go ahead and cry, Mandy. Let it all out."

Jake had been the last to console her before he was wrenched from her arms and carried, kicking and screaming, to the car that would drive him away from her. The car had turned a corner and Jake faded from view. Since then, her life consisted of corners to be bumped into and scraped against. It felt so good in his arms that for a moment, Miranda forgot just whose arms they were. "I'm sorry," she said, stiffening her back.

"Poor helpless kid. You try to act so strong like you're taking on the world."

Miranda twisted out of his arms.

He smiled with an indulgence that seemed out of character. Michaels smoothed the hair from her eyes, wiping the tears from her cheeks with a rumpled tissue fished from his pocket.

She felt like crying again. His tissue was dirty with ash from Ground Zero. *One day there will be nothing left of the Twin Towers, not one ash,* she thought.

"You have nothing to be sorry for, Mandy. You have every right to cry for your brother," he said.

She wished he wouldn't call her Mandy but didn't know how to tell him. A traitorous part of her did not want him to stop, the part yearning for intimacy. Miranda suddenly wished—what was it exactly she wished for?

Jake, she thought. *I want my brother to be alive like he was the last time I saw him with neither of us grown up and no years between us, and no death. I long for Mamma and Daddy and a family. I wish I had never grown up.*

Michaels lifted her chin, his eyes drilling into her.

She looked away, concentrating on pieces of skeletal walls rising up from the ashes in shapes of cathedral walls and crosses.

"I'm sure they appreciate you listening to all their names being called out, but it's not really necessary to hear the rest," he said, tapping her chin to gain attention.

"They appreciate my sacrifice? You mean the VIPs who are calling out the names? Of course they want a crowd to play to."

"I meant the fated ones."

"You think the dead are grateful for my being here? You, too, have quite an imagination," she said.

"We have two things in common then don't we? Come," he said, holding out his hand.

Miranda gripped his fingers.

Neither moved. They simply stared into each other's eyes, each taking the measure of the other.

A dimple dug into his cheek.

She returned his smile with a shy one of her own, feeling cuddly and warm like a kitten.

His eyebrows came together in a confused manner and he dropped her hand.

She buried her fists in her jacket pockets, hiding her trembling fingers. *I'm shivering because it upset me when they called Jake's name. I feel light-headed* from *crying.*

Michaels took her elbow, steering her away from the crowd and over to a secluded area. In the background they could hear the names of the dead being called out.

"Christ, it's going to take hours," he said, shoving his fist at the wall of a building.

She wanted to tell him to let his emotions out like he advised her, but he might break his hand against the wall.

Michaels might break the wall anyway.

"Fuck! Fuck! Fuck!" Finally, he stopped pounding. Michaels held his forehead against the wall, breathing heavily.

He yanked his flask from his pocket and took a few gulps.

"You've hurt yourself," she said, touching his abused hand.

Before she could examine his fist, he jerked his arm, shoving his hand in the pocket of his jacket. "Let's get out of here, Mandy. This place sickens me."

Miranda thought of patting his head the way he comforted her but twisted her hands behind her back. "Alright, Michaels, whatever you want."

He placed an arm across her shoulder, leaning against Miranda as she led him away from Ground Zero.

§

Chapter 13:1

And trust will be broken.

They walked northward in an eastern diagonal. She bit her tongue to keep from asking how badly he hurt his hand. Michaels did not appear to be in physical pain but spiritually, his face was as dark as the cloud following them. Some therapist he was, trying to get people to talk about their pain. Michaels should deal with his own wound instead of drowning his sorrows in a bottle.

I don't easily warm to people but I want to help Michaels, she thought. Before 9/11 a man with emotional baggage would have made her run the other way but Michaels was one of the survivors, and he was Jake's friend.

Up ahead was a facade of the Orient, marking China's claim to a speck of Manhattan shaped like a fortune cookie. If Chinatown cracked open, it would reveal the secrets of the Orient.

"You've got to taste one of these babies," Michaels said. He transformed from a man struggling in hell, to one who found heaven.

Miranda thought he referred to food eaten with chopsticks, but he stopped at a hot dog cart. It was only ten in the morning. Michaels ordered five dogs for himself, one for her and a bunless hot dog for Ashes. He smothered the dogs in mustard and relish, handing one to her and winking. "Uh, do you mind paying? I forgot my wallet," he said.

The hot dog was delicious but she eyed him with suspicion as he stuffed himself like a pig. "How long has it been since you've eaten one of these street delights spiced with taxi smog?"

"A couple of weeks or so. I usually buy a dog twice a week for lunch."

"So can we talk about Jake now?" she said.

"Can you smell that?" he said, inhaling deeply.

"More smog?" she said, wrinkling her nose.

"Nuts. My city."

"You said it," she said, tossing the wrapper in a can.

Michaels dragged her across the street to another vendor selling roasted nuts. He wolfed down a bag of these as well. "I love New York," he said with a full mouth. He shook his big head like a dog let into the house from the cold.

Miranda popped a nut in her mouth.

"It's hard to explain what I feel for my city. Manhattan perspires from ambition and the sweat of money," he said.

"I smell Eau de Manhattan toilet water. I don't know how anyone can live in a city dependent on public transportation."

"Here, traffic jams like a hard rock concert," he said, wiggling his hips.

Cab doors were slamming and cab drivers yelling. Horns honked in stuck traffic. Wanna-be passengers whistled at taxis. They snapped their fingers, yelled and pleaded. Obscenities flew in all directions.

"I miss my car," she said.

"You westerners and your damned cars," he snorted. "No wonder you're so fat. Uh, I didn't mean you."

"A car means freedom," she said, self-consciously smoothing her stomach down. She wasn't heavy but put on a couple of travel pounds.

"Cars pollute the world with your so-called freedom,"

"You do have a point. One point," she said, holding up her middle finger. "And how often have you been out West that you know so much?"

He grabbed her finger and bit lightly.

She yanked her finger from him, resisting the urge to lick her finger and taste him. *Get control before you make a fool of yourself!*

At her insistence they stopped at Columbus Park and sat on a bench. "I'm thinking of the ten hot dogs you consumed. You should let your food digest before we walk further," she said.

"Five. I just had five hot dogs."

"Just?" She grabbed his wrist. "How's your hand?"

Michaels jerked his hand from her, shoving his fist in his pocket.

"How close were you and Jake?" she said.

"Jacob's my best friend."

Miranda frowned at his use of the present tense, but she was reluctant to remind him that Jake was…gone. "How long did you know my brother?"

"I had my fortune read here once in Chinatown, not a canned fortune cookie but the real thing. An old Chinese man read my palm," he said.

Miranda sighed with frustration that Michaels changed the subject—again. "What did he reveal, this old Chinese man who was the real McCoy?"

"He was a Chan, not a McCoy."

"Smart ass," she said.

"Old man Chan said I would have a long, happy life filled with many children to burn incense for me after I'm dead. The Chinese believe a man should father many children to pray for him after he's deceased."

"And do you?"

"What?"

"Have any children?"

"No. Children would have been nice," he said in a voice filled with remorse.

"It's not too late."

"Are you volunteering to father my kids, Mandy?"

She blushed.

He leaned over and whispered into her ear.

She slapped his face.

He laughed meanly and said, "If I found you attractive, I never would have started this, promise or no promise, but as it is, you're the last woman on earth I would ask to be the mother of my child."

"This scar on my face is not hereditary," she said and walked away with her heart pounding painfully.

"Go comfort her," she heard him say to Ashes, and he sounded ashamed.

The little dog ran after her, nipping at her heels.

Miranda marched down the street. Ooh! No man ever spoke so obscenely to her before.

After two blocks, she felt more weary than mad. Her stomach churned and her head ached from his words—if I found you attractive, I never would have started this, promise or no promise.

What promise had Michaels made and to whom did he make it?

§

Chapter 14:1

Two jets hitting twin buildings
Is no accident.

Miranda walked aimlessly to Lower Midtown, near the East River. At the site of the United Nations she saluted the colors of the world, flags flown by member nations. "Perhaps men in there right now are plotting the fate of the world, the future of womankind, the way men always have in their arrogance to dominate," she mumbled to herself.

At the center of the complex was the Peace Bell, a gift from Japan cast from the coins of sixty nations. Miranda felt anything but peace.

Children would have been nice, Michaels had said, implying he was married but for some reason it was impossible for him and his wife to have kids. Miranda cringed that she ever brought up the subject. Her face still burned from his insult. *He is the biggest jerk I have ever met,* she thought.

Miranda had known plenty of jerks. She played symphonies with men, orchestrated with the wrong partner. There was just the physical, nothing lasting or earth shattering, just two bodies crashing in the night on their way to separate lives. She had several relationships lasting a few months but in the end parting, always parting.

In all fairness, Michaels never really made a pass at her and made it clear he would never want her.

Oh, God, why do I always desire men who don't want me?

Because you're unlovable, a voice whispered in her head. *There is something wrong with a man who would love you.*

Michaels wounded her pride, and she counted the cracks in the sidewalk. "One. Two. Step on a crack. Three. Four. Break Michaels' back."

Miranda hopped along, jumping on each crack. Last winter had been a cold one so the sidewalk resembled a road map.

"One. Two. Step on a crack. Three. Four. Break Michaels' back."

It began to sprinkle, and she snapped the umbrella open, hopping her way to the next street, feeling better with each crack she stepped on.

And feeling worse. *I'll never see him again. Why did I lose my temper and leave without learning about Jake?*

Ashes scampered ahead, playing in the puddles.

At a traffic light, Miranda heard footsteps running behind her.

Someone bumped into her and pushed her onto the street.

She landed with a thud on her back and lost her wind.

The pavement vibrated beneath her back. A noise like thunder rumbled in her ears.

She turned her head and stared with dazed eyes at a taxi barreling towards her.

§

Chapter 15:1

There will be heroes amongst us,
Both seen and invisible,
Vocal and silent.

Miranda twisted her head to where Ashes sat in the middle of the lane in the path of an oncoming taxi roaring towards them.

Ashes! I must get to Ashes! If anything happens to that poor, little dog…

She turned on her side to rise from the pavement.

Something landed on top of her.

Humph.

The world turned topsy-turvy, and she rolled like a ball until her shoulder slammed into the curb.

Her hair blew around her face as the taxi roared past her. Heat from the hot tires scorched her. Her tongue tasted like gasoline. She gasped for air and looked up, into the face of Michaels.

His face was grim, his eyes flashing a silver gray. He, too, was breathing heavily, but it wasn't because of his exertion. He inhaled her hair, groaning.

Miranda forgot about the pain in her shoulder. She was only aware of his hard body on top of hers; his chest crushed against her breasts; his hips digging into her flesh; and his leg shoved between her legs.

Her hands grasped his shoulders.

His muscles tensed beneath her fingers, his thighs quivering against her thighs.

Their feet were tangled.

Oh God, I should be shaken up because I nearly got killed just now. Instead, I feel more shaken because of him. She tried not to move because of his knee pressing between her legs, rising against the crotch of her jeans. His neck smelled of soap. The roughness of his face rubbed against her cheek, causing her to moan inwardly—she had just been thinking about how his not wanting her made her desire him.

Michaels lay perfectly still above her, not even seeming to breathe. He let out a deep sigh, rocking against her, proving to her that he did want her. His whole body cried out for it.

"I ache for you," Miranda thought she heard him say, but the words were like a feathery wisp in her ear.

He carefully rolled off her and yanked her onto the sidewalk.

"Thanks," she mumbled. Miranda was even more shocked when he kissed her forehead.

Oh my God, I can't think. What happened just now? What's happening? "Ashes? Where is Ashes?"

"Sh, the mutt's okay," he said, resting his chin on top of her head. "Your hair feels like silk. You smell of jasmine mixed with tar."

"A heady stink," she said, laughing self-consciously.

"Mandy," he murmured, resting his cheek on her hair. "Oh, Mandy."

The sound of her name being wrung from his throat made her respond like a mewing kitten.

He moaned and yanked her forward, crushing her breasts against his chest.

She hugged him back, pressing her body against him while his face snuggled into her collarbone, causing her to groan even louder. His lips were moist and left a trail of kisses up her neck, along the sensitive cord.

His tongue dived into her ear then circled the ear lobe. His breath was hot and she groaned deeply.

He pushed her against the wall and shoved his hands into her jacket, squeezing her waist.

He outlined her cheek bone with his tongue, sliding his hands across her back and pulling her shirt up until his hands scorched her skin.

Miranda swayed in his arms, her breath coming in little spurts.

He ran kisses across her chin, slowly moving his lips to her lips.

She licked his lips. His mouth smelled like peppermint, mingled with the odd odor of ashes from his cheek. His ears had the scent of burning metal. She sniffed his neck and the smell of Ground Zero assaulted her nostrils so she clung to him tighter, grinding her hips into his.

"You want me, don't you?" he said, breathing heavily.

Before she could answer, he moaned, "Oh God. No. No." He jerked his hands from under her shirt, wrenched her arms from around his waist, and pushed away from her. He bent over as if in pain.

She closed her eyes, running a trembling hand through her hair. It was hard to breathe, as if rubber bands engulfed her ribs.

He shoveled his fingers through his hair. Michaels seemed to be in his own hell. He hung his head, fighting for control and inhaling deeply.

She reached for him.

"Don't. Don't touch me," he said, holding a hand out in the same position a cop uses to stop traffic. "Don't stare at me all dreamy eyed. You should hate me."

She stood silently on wobbly legs, watching him shake the umbrella.

He cussed at the mechanism controlling the opening.

Miranda hugged her arms to her chest, feeling bereavement.

They both breathed like they ran a marathon and lost.

Her eyes drilled into his, watching, waiting, and pleading.

"I didn't mean for that to happen," he stammered and he pulled out that damned flask again and took a drink.

"Fuck," he said and threw the empty flask on the sidewalk.

Miranda felt like crying as she huddled beneath the oversized umbrella, taking cover from the rain and him. They were so close yet far, together yet alone.

All she could smell was the scent of peaches wafting from his hair.

All she could taste was his chin that had scraped against her lips like sandpaper.

All she could feel was the swelling of her own desire. Things were getting out of hand. She slapped him thirty minutes ago. Unbelievable! She falls into his arms because he pushes her out of the way of a cab. You're my hero, Miranda wanted to say, but didn't want to risk sounding like a teenager. Don't make any waves, she always told herself. Play it safe. Yet all she could hear was the roaring in her ears from his lips that still rocked her like the ocean. She was the tidal wave gravitating towards him, then receding, unsure if she was really welcome. Miranda oscillated between desire and insanity, ecstasy and despair.

I didn't mean for that to happen, he had said. Don't touch me.

"We just got caught up in the moment," she said in a dull voice. "Believe me, it won't happen again." She buttoned up her jacket with shaky fingers. The result was that the buttons did not match the holes and her jacket was higher on the left than on the right, but her appearance was the least of her worries.

Miranda arched her back, rubbing her sore shoulder. "What happened?" she said, mainly to make conversation at an awkward moment.

"You must have tripped and fallen into the street like a dumb, clumsy California ox," he snapped. Michaels snorted, like he was disgusted with himself for having kissed her.

He hurt her feelings purposefully, as if he wanted her to cry. Michaels goaded her into shedding tears. Well, she wouldn't give him the satisfaction. Her shoulder hurt like hell, but she would not cry in front of him.

"No. I think someone pushed me," she insisted, trying to keep a rein on her temper. Michaels was so frustrating, the way he pushed her away from him. Miranda spoiled for a fight, even though it had been the sensible thing for him to do, given that they were smack dab in the middle of a crowd. Neither had been aware of people around them then. They had kissed in a dream-like setting where time stands still, and everything moves in slow motion. Even now, Miranda could not hear what was happening around her. She was only aware of Michaels. There was no one else, in a dream, in a nightmare, or on the street. "Did you see who pushed me?" she said.

"I've got better things to do with my time than keep an eye on you," he said in a tone of voice like he wouldn't mind putting on the gloves with her and duking it out.

Where had Michaels come from—seemingly out of nowhere? Funny, he didn't look the part of a guardian angel. There was more the devil about the man.

Awareness slowly returned in bits and painful pieces. Where in the heck had her purse gone? Thank goodness she had traveler's checks.

Ah, he was standing on her purse.

"Excuse me," she said and bent down to pick up her purse which was open. None of her belongings were scattered about so she snapped her purse shut, hoping nothing was missing. Miranda was damned if she was going to search through her purse with him looking over her shoulder, sneering at her.

She did take out a compact mirror to examine a cut on her lip, or did Michaels do that to her?

"Maybe we should get you to a hospital," he said in an anxious voice. He reached out a finger to touch a scrape on her forehead.

She tossed her head so he couldn't touch her. "I'm not feeling puny. Just need to catch my breath is all," she said, *and my sanity. I must have been crazy to want you, even for a minute.*

"Are you sure?" he said. The look in his eyes claimed he had some feeling for her, at least because she was a human being.

"I do feel nauseous," she admitted in a tired voice. *You make me feel sick.*

"Here, hold your head between your legs," he said, pulling her down to the curb.

Miranda rested a few minutes until the sickness passed. She was relieved the feelings her traitorous body felt when he laid on top of her, also passed.

He squeezed her neck, massaging her skin with his big, hot, callused hand.

Miranda moaned and jerked her head away. She massaged her neck to erase his fingerprints. "It's possible you saved my life," she grudgingly admitted.

Michaels shrugged his shoulders like it was nothing.

I feel so guilty for wanting to break his back. She giggled at her childish thoughts of revenge. Guilt did not lessen her resentment of how his touch made her feel or when he called her Mandy, like they were childhood friends. Miranda never in her life felt so many emotions towards one man. In the space of a few days she felt hope, fear, dread, anger, excitement, and dislike. She was motivated by panic, guilt, frustration, resentment, hatred, and desire. Passion frightened her the most. His masculinity made her too aware of her femininity. Contrarily, she felt like hitting him. By nature, Miranda was not violent but Michaels magnified all her emotions. He made her feel inadequate. She apologized more to him than to anyone in her life, and actually begged him. She was more curious about Michaels than any other man of her acquaintance and longed to ask all sorts of personal questions, but was worried he would get the wrong idea, especially since Miranda wasn't sure why she cared to know.

In the future, I'll maintain an aloof manner and put bits and pieces of him together from things he says.

There, Miranda felt better because she had a plan.

Oh, damn. She especially wanted to know why he was the one who kissed her and then demanded she not touch him. Was her touch so disgusting to him? Miranda was appalled at what happened between them. If he had not shoved her away, she probably would have invited him up to her hotel room.

You still can, her heart whispered.

No, never, remember? He didn't mean for any of it to happen. I'm not his type.

Her stomach churned and her head spun. She didn't want him to see her so helpless and weak.

He raised an eyebrow at her dirty clothes.

Before Miranda could react, he dusted her off. He reached around for her buttocks, and she jumped back. "I'm a mess," she squeaked, sweeping her hands across her rear.

"You look fine, just exhausted."

"I haven't been sleeping well," she confessed, rubbing the dark circles under her eyes.

"The city's been taking its toll on you. Manhattan doesn't take to outsiders."

I'm not an outsider, she wanted to scream. *Look at me, Michaels. I can take anything you and your damned city dish out. See this knife scar on my cheek? You should see the girl who gave it to me.*

"You should go back to your hotel and rest," he suggested and didn't wait for her answer. "Taxi," he yelled, holding up a hand to a cab that came screeching to a halt.

I am an outsider, point taken. Michaels gets a cab on the first try.

Miranda made a dirty finger with both hands, aiming them at his back, but the gesture did not make her feel good like when she lived at the juvenile detention home, flipping everyone off.

Michaels took her hand and she limped beside him to the cab. He was strong and she felt safe beside him. Contrarily, her resentment boiled because his strength made her feel weak and unsafe with him, not because Miranda didn't trust him but because she didn't trust herself.

Michaels was gentle with her and took great care as he helped Miranda into the cab. He refused the stolen umbrella. "You'll need it when you get to your hotel," he said, swallowing.

He stood with the door open and his ragged shoe resting against the cab.

Ashes jumped across her lap but she ignored the dog. Miranda stared up at Michaels and waited because he acted like he wanted to say something. He kept opening his mouth and closing it. Finally he said, "It's over. I won't be back. I can't come back. I'm getting too involved. It's a mess, Mandy."

"I don't understand."

"Good night," he said, shutting the cab door and placing a barrier between them.

The rain patted his head, dripping down his face, but he paid the rain no heed. Michaels stood with his hands clenched into fists, watching her cab drive away.

She looked out the back window until his face became a dot.

Michaels looked so vulnerable, with such a lonely look in his bloodshot eyes. It had taken all her will power not to ask him to go back to the Algonquin with her.

Just so he can get a good night's sleep and a hot meal. I swear Michaels looks as if he is homeless.

I'll never see him again.

"Oh, Ashes, I forgot to ask him where Jake lived."

The dog whined, sensing her mood.

It's for the best, she thought, feeling a sense of relief that she would not see Michaels again.

Yet, Miranda felt a yearning, like she lost something she could never truly have.

It's just Jake. I had such high hopes of finding out about my brother. Oh, Jake, I am a mess!

§

Chapter 16:1

And the senses will heighten
To every danger,
Every foe,
Both seen
And unseen.

The Algonquin was an old-fashioned, turn-of-the-20th-Century hotel, with a big brassy key that must have fallen from her purse when it spilled onto the sidewalk.

The desk manager gave Miranda a spare.

Though it was after midnight and technically Sunday, she sat at the Blue Bar and ordered a decanter of wine.

She clicked her fingernails on the bar counter, feeling the sensation of someone watching her. She eyed the patrons tossing off Manhattans, beers and assorted other drinks. There were a few couples, another lone woman, and eight men.

No one met her eyes nor sent out any vibes, yet she felt eyes on her.

Miranda guzzled the wine in her glass, and slammed some bills on the counter. She grabbed a full decanter and glass, and exited the bar.

She scooped up Ashes from outside and hid him under her coat. He wouldn't make much of a guard dog but at least Ashes could yap.

Miranda looked around the elevator. No one followed.

I'm being silly, she thought. She stepped into the elevator and peeked out.

A man dressed in a conservative business suit entered the elevator and punched the twelfth floor, her floor.

When the elevator doors opened, she whistled softly while he exited first.

What a relief! He turned in the opposite direction.

"Sit," she said, setting Ashes and the decanter on the hall floor.

He wagged his tail, smiling at her.

Miranda balanced the wine glass in one hand while unlocking the room door.

Ashes scurried into the room, nearly tripping her.

He rolled on the bed, his tongue hanging out.

She kicked off her shoes and filled the glass with wine, emptying the decanter. Miranda toasted herself in the dresser mirror, tossed her head back and guzzled the wine. She rarely drank. A few sips more and she floated drunkenly. Her reward for imbibing was numbness.

She flopped down on the bed with the nagging feeling that her life was spinning out of control, just like the room.

Miranda drifted into a mindless sleep.

When she woke up, her throbbing head was nothing compared to her achiness from falling in the street. The left side of her body hurt from her neck down to her ankle. She popped a few acetaminophens.

Damn city. Damn Michaels.

Moonlight shone through the bay window. *A full moon,* she thought, snorting. *How romantic. All I need are candles.*

A mindless movie on cable flickered across the screen, an action thriller with a dumb hunk who couldn't act his way out of a closet.

Jake—Michaels has told me little about my brother, she thought.

Hot water from a shower massaged her soreness.

Her body was ultra-sensitive to the fluffy threads of the towel.

She cocked her head at her naked body, turning half-way to the full length mirror and arching her back. She reached a hand behind and pushed.

He had touched her here, here, and there.

She ran her fingers down her neck with a feathery touch.

His lips were on her shoulder, neck, and cheekbone.

In my ear.

Miranda closed her eyes and his hot tongue filled her, consuming her with desire.

She softly ran the back of her hand across her cheek bone and chin.

She swept her hands across her breasts and imagined Michaels touching her.

Her fingers traveled downward, circling her belly button before moving to her center, the connecting point of her tingling nerves.

Miranda swayed and her hair swept her back in a sensuous motion reminding her of his fingers.

His knee had been here.

She stroked herself and rocked.

She groaned, reaching out a hand to cling to the sink.

"Michaels," she moaned, in half ecstasy and half self-loathing.

A voice whispered in her ear—Mandy.

She could feel his hot breath, his moist tongue.

She groaned.

This is crazy.

No it isn't. There is nothing wrong with a fantasy. An imaginary man can't hurt me.

Miranda jerked her white nightgown over her head, brushed her teeth, and stuck her tongue out at her shiny-clean face in the mirror, looking like a little girl ready for bed.

Ashes sat on the covers with a hang-dog look, as though he knew what she had been up to. His ears pricked up. He had heard.

She blushed, and threw a pillow at him.

Miranda flopped on the bed, smiling at the ceiling. Maybe she could get a good night's sleep now. For the first time since coming to this city she felt relaxed.

"What? What?" she mumbled, half-asleep.

A husky voice was laughing.

Miranda rubbed her damp neck and yawned. Her neighbors next door sure kept late hours.

There it was again, laughter. The hotel had thin walls.

The laughter's coming from my room! My missing room key! Someone was following me, watching me!

She reached out a hand to the end table, searching for her cell phone.

Crap!

Her cell phone tumbled to the carpet.

§

Chapter 17:1

Terror lurks beneath the covers.

The laughter in her room grew louder.

Her heart fluttered. Miranda reached for the hotel phone, and grabbed the mouth piece.

The cord dangled—the dialer had been removed while she slept!

Someone followed me to the Algonquin and entered the room with my missing key while I slept like a drunk. Oh, God! Please, please protect me!

She grabbed a table knife from the night stand. Miranda was shaking so badly, she almost knocked over the lamp as she reached for the light switch.

The dead bolt and chain lock were in place.

Maybe the trespasser relocked the door behind him.

Her heart screeched to a halt—the tail of her blouse hanging in the closet moved slightly.

She released her breath slowly, trying to gain control. *Don't panic. It's only the air conditioner blowing air in the direct path of the closet.*

Miranda lifted one leg over the mattress, feeling the side of the bed with her heel. It would be impossible for an intruder to crawl under the inch or two of space under the bed.

The bathroom door was open.

Miranda crept out of bed, holding the knife to her ear, ready to stab a prowler.

When I peed before going to bed, the shower curtain had been open.

The shower curtain was still open and the bathroom unoccupied.

She leaned against the bathroom wall, her knees weak with relief.

Her heart screeched to a halt—there. She swung her head toward the room window and the sound of laughter. This time she could pinpoint the direction of the sound. It was the strangest laughter she ever heard and came from the bay window of her room.

Miranda breathed a sigh of relief. At least the noise wasn't coming from the closet.

Knock. Knock.

The window, she thought with shock. Her room was way up on the twelfth floor with no patio extension. In fact, the windows didn't even open.

Yet once again there was a knocking and laughter echoed from the window, only the laughter sounded more like musical notes being played through a wind tunnel.

She tiptoed towards the tinkling laughter, sounding like ice bumping against a glass. The laughter sounded other-worldly.

Miranda threw the sheers aside and yanked the knife from behind her back, ready to jab.

Jake floated outside her window. He had the saddest expression.

He put his palm against the window.

Miranda placed her hand against his, the pane separating them.

"I'll let you in," she said loudly.

The window would not open.

He lifted a finger to the pane and wrote, using moisture from the window.

Her pulse pounded as she read the letters D A E D.

Suddenly, a rush of frigid air blew against her face even though the window was sealed shut. Her hair blew wildly and she was pushed from the cold window pane.

Then just as abruptly, the wind stopped and there was a whoosh.

The resulting silence was as eerie as his laughter had been.

Jake was gone, leaving his message that made no sense as a word.

She outlined each letter. *What was Jake trying to say? What was Jake trying to say? What was…?*

The letters faded and the window pane cleared of moisture.

She placed her face against the cold glass, a lone tear sliding down her cheek.

Miranda pulled the sheers and curtains together with trembling fingers.

She climbed into bed on wobbly legs, yanking the covers up to her chin.

She rubbed her icy feet together, but couldn't warm up in a room like a tomb. The temperature before Jake's visit had been tropical and was now arctic.

No way am I getting out of bed to mess with the thermostat.

She flipped on the television and watched a snowy screen. The static buzz coming from the set lulled her to sleep.

Miranda dreamt of *running through Manhattan streets with Jake until he shot up in the air. He danced on the roof of a skyscraper.*

She yelled up from the street for him to come down and be with her.

He laughed in her ear.

Jake balanced from the roof of the Algonquin, threatening to jump.

Ashes appeared beside Jake, yapping.

She woke up, hugging Ashes and crying into his fur. She had worried more about the dog than Jake.

My brother is, after all, a fantasy, she thought as she drifted back to sleep.

The mattress creaked.

Jake?

Miranda patted the bed but no one was there, yet she rolled from a heavier weight on the driver's side.

Now why would I think, driver, she thought, half-awake and half-asleep.

The smell of Old Spice Cologne enveloped the bed, along with a deep sigh.

Miranda was completely awake now; her eyes frozen open and her mouth open in a silent scream. She remembered the ghost from her dream, where Jake danced along the top of a train. An invisible man had stood behind her, smelling of Old Spice. She had later smelled Old Spice coming from a ghost sitting on her bed.

He's back!

She whimpered with fear while a hand slid up her thigh to her stomach, circling her belly like it was a steering wheel.

Miranda grabbed the hand touching her stomach but grasped air.

Lips nuzzled her neck and the line of her jaw.

Bed bugs! Oh, God, let it be bed bugs!

She patted her face and neck, panicking. Those had been human lips kissing her! Invisible lips! Ghost lips!

A bare leg covered hers and she itched from the sprinkling of hair.

God, help me!

She buckled, trying to throw the ghost off her.

Arms pressed beside her head, trapping Miranda.

She smelled soap and smoldering ashes, along with Old Spice.

A nose rubbed against her nose and hair brushed her cheeks.

"No," she said with chattering teeth. "Go away!"

A voiced groaned into her ear.

Holy shit! I'm going to be raped by a ghost!

Help me, a voice whispered.

"Fuck off!" she yelled. "Leave me alone!"

A tongue dived into her ear.

Miranda screamed.

Whoosh! The room grew frigidly cold.

She sensed the presence was gone.

Miranda sat up, hot and sweating.

She snapped on the light but no one was there except Ashes snoring under the bed.

Yet once again, she felt like someone was watching her.

Miranda left the light on and turned on her side.

Only at the crack of dawn, did she feel safe enough to close her eyes.

§

Chapter 18:1

And confusion will rule.

Sunday Morning, September 23, 2001

Miranda sighed at her hair that always misbehaved. She was not so bad looking, nor did she care to look like a plastic model. Her face had character at least, especially her scar, or lack of character, if the truth ever be told.

She was no longer that wild child.

Miranda knocked her forehead against the mirror. It had taken years to like herself, after beatings in foster homes. Good for nothing they called her. The caseworker never explained exactly what she did wrong or why she was unwanted.

Now Michaels comes along and tramples my self-confidence.

Jake. I should think of Jake.

She did not travel all this way to have her feelings hurt by Michaels. She didn't need his so-called help. "If only Jake would talk during his supernatural visits and tell me his address. Dammit!" Miranda swept her arm across the bathroom counter. Makeup, perfume, lotion and pain killers crashed to the floor.

She picked up her tennis shoes, pounding the soles together—ashes swirling in the air.

Her brother's face formed in Ground Zero dust that had been trapped in the grooves of her shoes. His dusty face twisted like a tornado. Jake opened his mouth as if to speak but all he managed to do was look panicked.

Miranda tried to comfort Jake, but the ashes dissipated, intermixing with dust mites and bathroom deodorant.

She slapped, grabbed, and waved at the air, but could not touch her brother.

She slumped against the wall, her shoulders shaking with sobs.

Ashes barked and jumped into her arms. She hugged the little dog. "You are a comfort."

They exited the hotel and she uncovered the dog. Ashes stood between her legs, wagging his tail with his tongue hanging out and one ear flopping behind his head. Alfie, the doorman, was a dog lover and never gave her a hard time about Ashes.

Miranda brooded at the curb, waiting for a taxi.

She took out a pad of paper and pen to decipher Jake's message. *Let's see, he wrote daed, which makes no sense. Juggling the letters makes the word dade, which could be the street he lived on.* The letters could be the initials of four words. *His location,* she thought excitedly then frowned, thinking none of the letters related to the area of Ground Zero. *Is Jake still alive or is he trying to tell me where his remains are? Or, switching the two middle letters makes the word, dead.* Heaviness descended on her shoulders—*Jake is trying to tell me he is dead.*

"Mandy?"

She turned and was shocked by Michaels leaning against the wall under the hotel canopy. He gave her a sad sort of smile, lifting his hand in a half-hearted wave. Michaels was rumpled as though he slept in his clothes. His face was unshaven. He looked hung over, his face a mask of pain.

"Where did you come from?" she said in a tiny voice, her lips trembling. She struggled to hold herself together. *I can't cry in front of him. Not again.*

"I've been here all night," he said.

Thankful for the distraction, she closed her eyes, imagining him in an alley sleeping under a big cardboard box with the rest of the homeless.

Quit feeling sorry for him! What a liar! He probably spent the night with his wife. Maybe he is really rich—one of those crazies who pretends he isn't.

Miranda was in no mood for jokes or teasing flirtations with a man who waffled like a bad cable connection. Nor was she in a humor to encourage a man who drove her to drink.

"I couldn't wait to see you again," he said, shrugging his shoulders.

"Yeah, right. You should try another pickup line, Sherlock."

"Woke up on the wrong side of the bed have we?" he said, spitting in the way men do when they've hit their mark.

"Have we?" she said and raised an eyebrow.

Michaels looked like he slept in the wrong bed. His face was haggard and paler than usual. Gone was his sharp Wall Street look of confidence. His hair was rumpled, as if he spent several hours pulling at his scalp. If anything, his messiness made him look more attractive, more human, and not as robotic. His being wrinkled made him more approachable. Michaels had always dressed in slacks with a crease so crisp it might cut her if she rubbed her hand down his thigh. Miranda reddened at the thought of touching him. No way would she dare. Like anyone who ever played with paper, she experienced cuts before, tiny slits barely visible that hurt like hell.

Yet, she stifled the urge to straighten his hair.

Don't touch me—he had said.

She rode a roller coaster with this man, the way his emotions swung like a pendulum, and she had to swing out of the way lest he punch her.

But…he still needs to tell me about Jake.

Without asking if he could join her, Michaels climbed into the cab Alfie managed to halt.

The very proper English Alfie should have been a barrister. He gave the cabbie the third degree about prices, safety, and directions for where Miranda wanted to go. "You better not go the long way, Chum, and cheat this nice lady who's visiting. She's a guest at the Algonquin and when she returns, I'm going to ask her what fee you charged. If you cheated her, I'm reporting you."

Alfie took out pad and pencil, recording the cabbie stats and his yellow apparatus of transportation, which is how he referred to New York City taxis.

Alfie safely tucked Miranda into the cab, and she handsomely tipped him for his services.

The cab was a third-world country. Foreign music screeched from a radio with no knobs. Pine trees dangled from a rear view mirror promising mountain fresh scent but delivering stink of curry. A scratched sliding glass window divided passenger from immigrant who learned to drive with video game. The seats were worn.

Michaels narrowed his eyes to where Miranda huddled in the opposite corner. "You push yourself any more into that upholstery, Lady, and you're going to wind up in the trunk. We could have taken separate cabs," he barked.

"Don't be childish. I got little sleep last night. I'm just trying to get comfortable," she said, cursing herself for even speaking to him.

He raised an eyebrow and snapped his head to look at the opposite window.

She snuck a peek at his profile. He was ruggedly handsome and totally male. There was an intimacy about his messiness, like he just rose from bed. This cab was too small for the two of them. She tore her eyes from him, looking the other way.

"Did you have a good evening, Princess?" he said, sighing and rubbing his ear in that manner he had when nervous.

"Yes," she said a bit too quickly and guiltily. She blushed and shyly stared out the window. A dab of a smile quivered her lips. *If he asks why I'll laugh.*

"Any soreness?" he said.

"What," she said, opening her eyes wide.

"From falling yesterday."

"Oh that. I had a hot shower and took some aspirin. I'm a bit stiff but otherwise okay," she said, sniffling. Miranda didn't dare tell him his city gave her a slight cold and was kicking her ass. Maybe she was allergic to Manhattan—an allergy is your environment rejecting you like a parasite.

Michaels had kissed her and maybe she gave him her cold. "Are you okay?" she said.

He shrugged his shoulders, ignoring her coughing and sneezing. Michaels stared out the window with a gloomy face and bleak eyes.

They were headed in a northeasterly direction. The city flashed in a repetitive scene of tall buildings and pavement.

"Wait. Stop here," he yelled.

The cab came to a squealing halt.

"There," Michaels said, pointing a finger.

"What?"

"That's my apartment."

Ah, so he does have a home.

His apartment building resembled most other Manhattan buildings, straight up, made of mortar, brick, windows and too little living space. There was a minuscule amount of parking space, too much smog, and too much traffic passing by. His apartment was close enough to a subway stop both for convenience and annoyance.

"What floor do you live on?" she asked.

"Thirty-ninth."

She counted the floors and reached the fifteenth when Michaels ordered the cabbie to, "Drive on."

Miranda was curious as hell about his apartment and to see how he lived, but she would not invite herself in.

Michaels hung his head out the cab window, salivating at his apartment building.

"Where did Jake live?" she said flippantly.

He swung his head around with his mouth hanging open. If she wasn't so frustrated, his expression would have been comical—Michaels looked as if he was caught with his hand in a cookie jar. "Don't remember," he grudgingly admitted.

"You don't remember where my brother lived? Your best friend?"

"I guess that's about right," he said, rubbing his forehead and pulling at his nose.

"Exactly, who are you?" she said with a rush of air.

§

Chapter 19:1

In churches they will pray.
Across all lands
People will pray for deliverance.

Michaels gave her an exasperated look.

Their eyes locked, each taking the measure of the other.

She tightened her fists, her nails digging painfully into her palms.

He flexed his hands open, pointing his fingers to ten different ways to explain who he was. "I'm who I said I am," he hollered. Michaels hesitated before continuing in a calmer voice. "It's just that I have these blackouts ever since I hit my head. Then something fell from the ceiling. My memory comes and goes. For instance, I forget to eat," he said, looking out the window and frowning. "And I forget my wallet."

There was a catch to his voice, and she touched his arm. "Oh, Michaels, have you seen a doctor for these blackouts?"

"I have a concussion. The doctor said the memory problem is temporary and should clear up eventually. The doctor said not to push me to remember. My head hurts if you press me," he said, clearing his throat. He must be embarrassed by his condition. Michaels looked at the floor and not at her.

The cab stopped and the driver jumped out. "Here we are," he said, opening the door for her.

"I didn't ask you to bring me here."

"Your man did," he said, holding out his hand for the fare.

"He's not my man. Ask him to pay you since this place was his idea."

"I, uh, forgot my wallet," Michaels said.

"Oh, you're not carrying that old beat up thing that looks like it's filled with moths?" she said.

Michaels turned his back to her. His shoulders were stiff.

She paid for the hot dogs yesterday, too. Miranda slapped some bills into the cabbie's hand and the driver sped away, as if he feared she would change her mind about the fare.

"So, where to?" she said, glaring.

"Church, to pray for your soul," Michaels said, chuckling at her look of dismay which seemed to restore his good humor.

"Perhaps a morning in church would help you," she said.

"I look like a lost soul, do I? Well don't waste your breath on me."

"Why? Are you too far gone?"

"A good woman might redeem me," he said, wiggling his brows.

"Don't waste your breath on me either," she snorted.

"Why? Are you a bad woman, Mandy?"

"Sometimes," she admitted.

"I'd like to hear your confession about being bad," he said, laughing.

"Father Michaels? I don't think so," she said, looking up at the impressive twin steeples of St. Patrick's Cathedral. "Why a Catholic church?"

"I figured you must have been baptized by a priest," he said.

Her heart skipped a beat because he would only know this from Jake. "Was Jake religious? Did my brother still believe in God?"

"How the heck would I know? Church isn't exactly something guys talk about when hanging out at a bar," he said, shrugging his shoulders.

"Touché, but you do discuss religion with women and even have the gall to drag me to church against my will."

"Tut. Tut. I didn't exactly handcuff you."

"More like kidnap. And you are what religion? Catholic?"

"I always worshipped money. Stay," he ordered Ashes and held the door of St. Patrick's Cathedral wide open.

"But I'm not Catholic," she hissed and he pushed her in.

"Me neither. Not anymore," he said, slamming the door. "I don't see the papist police checking IDs today so I think it's safe for us to be here."

"I used to be Catholic. We'll only stay a minute," she said and picked up a pamphlet giving the cathedral history. "How gothic," she murmured in appreciation. The hunchback of St. Patrick's Cathedral must be hiding behind one of the twin white peaks skyrocketing to the heavens with a cross atop each for good measure.

"It took a lot of passing around the basket to build this baby," Michaels said, whistling.

They entered through massive bronze doors and stood at the back because all seats were taken since 9/11.

The 9:30 mass was well underway, and the priest was poking his sticky fingers down people's throats. Communion was being served.

Miranda had never seen so many saints, even the doors were carved with them. The statues of saints which adorned the cathedral seemed to be staring at her, and making her feel guilty for not having gone to church in years.

St. Patrick's was filled with a musky odor of mystical herbs and spices begging the age old question—why exactly are we here? For what purpose was man put on earth? And where do we go from here? Miranda's pulse pounded with questions about Jake.

Let's see. My last confession was so long ago, I don't remember the words.

She bowed her head, entwining her hands. *Why Jake, God? My brother didn't do anything wrong, that I'm aware of. The good die young or so the saying goes. It's me who is the sinner.*

Pray for me, Jake, so that I won't end up in hell like I was told by all those strangers who never understood me. Pray for me. And pray for Michaels so that he'll get better and remember before I have to leave.

"My family! I don't want them to see me!" Michaels yanked her from the pew, dragging her towards the exit.

"Why ever not?" she said loudly so that those in the back of the church turned their heads and looked at her with scolding faces.

She craned her neck to get a better view of the parade marching down the aisle, the Catholics who received communion. Which of these religious paragons were related to Michaels? They all had a self-righteous look. Maybe they were all related, and this was the Michaels' clan come to church on a Sunday morn, minus the black sheep of the family.

He leaned against the wall, trying to catch his breath outside the church in the sinful air. "Oh, God. Oh, God," he said like he was choking.

Tears streamed down his cheeks.

"What's going on, Michaels? Why are you hiding from your family?"

§

Chapter 20:1

And imaginations will run wild with fear.

"I don't want my mother to see I've been drinking on a Sunday. It's an ongoing battle between us. You know, my family actually had an intervention? But I stormed out and haven't seen them since. She thinks a priest can get me to give up booze, but Catholic school left a rancid taste in my mouth," Michaels said with a smile that was more a crack across his face.

"You claimed to be religious," she said, reminding him with flashing eyes of his lecture to her on Friday. "You were preaching bullshit."

"I said I believe in God. I never, ever said I went to church."

"Your family would resent you spending so much time with me," she said, narrowing her eyes.

"On the contrary, my family would feel sorry for you having to put up with the likes of me," he said woefully.

Why, because he hid from a wife? A beloved daughter-in-law? *Children*, she thought with slumped shoulders. *This would explain his vanishing act.* "You seem to have a lot of freedom," she said.

"It must be hard, being a woman all alone in the world," he said. His words were a simple observation, spoken with so much emotion. Here she was all alone with a man she barely knew, walking in an unfamiliar city. If anything happened to her, no one would ever know she was with Michaels.

In her imagination, *Michaels jerks her into an alley and yanks up her skirt. He runs his hand up her leg and squeezes. Groaning, he smashes her lips with his and shoves his tongue down her throat.*

His fingers outline the band of her underpants.

Groping.

Massaging.

Invading.

Savageness turns to caressing. His tongue outlines her lips in a slow, sensuous circle. His mouth is gentle as he pecks at her lips with butterfly kisses. With his thumb he traces her jaw.

Her own hand reaches out and grabs at the buckle of his pants. Her fingers fumble in the dark. She moans.

She moans?

Miranda groaned and stomped her foot. "Why do you say that about me being alone?"

"A woman with no husband, father or brother brings out protective instincts in a man," he said, rolling his eyes.

"Or the predator drawn to a helpless female."

"You are a force to be reckoned with. Come now," he said, smiling lazily. "Surely you don't see me as a predator."

"I'm not so sure," she said, biting her lip and examining him through half-closed eyes.

"If you're lucky enough to have me, my Lady, it will be at my invitation," he said, lifting her hand and kissing her wrist like an old-fashioned gentleman.

"You sound sure of yourself," she said, snorting.

"Because you already have," he said, licking her wrist. His tongue slid beneath the arm of her jacket.

Some gentleman. God help me. Here's the animal that first approached me at Ground Zero when I wondered how sane I was to follow him.

Miranda jerked her trembling fingers from his grasp. She walked with her head bowed and her hands buried in her jacket pockets.

She heard just her own heels clicking against the sidewalk and Ashes beside her. *He can go to hell. Arrogant asshole.*

He saved your life yesterday when you were pushed into the street, a voice whispered in her head.

Oh shut up. Michaels hands me a crumb about Jake every now and then and I let down my guard.

After a few minutes she realized a car followed her. Miranda swung her head to a yellow cab zigzagging and bouncing across the potholes. Michaels dwarfed the back seat. "Get in," he ordered in a tense voice.

She ignored him.

"Don't be an idiot! It's going to rain, and it's a long way to Central Park from Fifth Avenue and Fifty-Fifth Street," he said.

"I'm only going with you because of Ashes," she said. "And who says we're going to Central Park?"

Michaels grinned like a little boy who just got his way.

Miranda couldn't shake the images from her mind of him dragging her into the nearest alley. The air in the cab was confining. Miranda gulped a few breaths, feeling like she suffocated. She must not, under any circumstances, ever invite him to her hotel. Nor should she drink around him and lose her senses. Miranda participated in the monthly girls' night out where she sat at a bar nursing a drink, making small talk with nondescript men, some of whom she dated but never warmed up to. This man from Ground Zero would burn her. She would only make a fool of herself.

Don't be so dramatic. You haven't made a fool of yourself, a voice whispered in her head.

The day is not yet over.

Jump out of the cab while you still can!

But…what of Jake?

No! I have to play this out to the end. It's too late now. It was too late the moment Michaels told me he was Jake's friend.

But his blackouts and his missing—what? Years? Months? Weeks? Days? Hours? How big is his memory gap? Has Michaels forgotten tidbits of Jake's life or a smorgasbord? I must be patient, he said.

Jake.

But, it wasn't Jake's face she saw when Miranda closed her eyes. Next, she would be imagining Michaels in the shower with his clothes off. Miranda blushed. *He has a good body. In fact, I've never seen a man look so good in a pair of slacks and a polo shirt. His shoulders are broad and his waist small. He's got a nice butt.*

Mm, imagine him naked in the shower with water dripping down his chest to the middle...

She gulped. *Don't focus on that part of his body. Hanging around Michaels is contagious, which is why I imagined us together. It's all this sexual tension. His looks and insinuations. His teasing and kissing me yesterday. Any red-blooded woman would daydream around a sexy man like Michaels. Well you better wake up, Miranda.*

"I'm sorry for my moodiness," she said, holding out her hand to him.

"You are an aggravating woman," he said, shaking her hand.

He did not let go of her hand and she blushed, hoping her thoughts didn't show on her face. She sensed real chemistry between them, the attraction of negative and positive loins. Miranda squirmed against the seat, causing the upholstery to creak, making her jump. She jerked her hand away.

"Don't worry, Mandy, I don't intend to ravish you in the back seat of a cab. You're different from any of the women I've known," he said, flatly.

"I just don't want to be one of your blackouts," she said.

"And you think I have many?"

She nodded her head.

"I will never forget you," he said.

"You say that like I'll never see you again."

"We are simply two cabs that pass in the night. You'll go back to Los Angeles. Probably meet some boring man with a beer belly who proudly goes by the name of Bubba from Buda, California. You'll get married and buy matching pickups. Bubba will keep you barefoot and pregnant." He stared out the window, clamping his lips closed. He opened his mouth, but whatever he had to say seemed difficult. "And I...," he began, hesitating.

"Yes?" she said. *You have a wife stashed at your apartment barefoot and pregnant? Oh I forgot. She's a sophisticated New Yorker who probably just left church and is headed the other direction of Fifth Avenue to shop for a three-piece suit to wear at her job in a high-powered New York office, where she's running the frigging world.*

"My time is, also, limited," he said.

"Your time?"

He stared out the cab window, the silence between them seeming as painful to him as it was to her.

Oh, God, she was falling for him.

I didn't mean for that to happen. Don't touch me, he had said.

But Michaels had touched her, storming through her defenses.

It's just because he knew Jake that I want to get close to Michaels.

Perhaps I'm wrong about this thing being about a wife. Maybe his injury is greater than he let on. He has blackouts because his brain is injured and irreparably damaged. He'll just continue to deteriorate until...

Or maybe he has cirrhosis of the liver from all that drinking. He said his time is limited.

Or maybe he has a brain tumor.

She hugged her chest, rocking. *He can't die.*

Michaels ignored her and stared out the window.

He's keeping something from me.

§

Chapter 21:1

And life will go on.

"When you visit Manhattan, you have to eat Sunday brunch at Tavern on the Green in Central Park," Michaels said.

Miranda agreed the wait was worth it, especially the topiary garden. Animals carved out of shrubbery were so realistic, it seemed the leaf-draped ape would pound his chest, run screaming through Central Park, and climb the Empire State Building rising to the south.

Ashes hid between the front legs of a giant topiary bunny while they sat at a bar made from dead trees. Sunday morning was an odd time to be drinking a glass of blood-red wine, but the breakfast wine was a concoction of cranberry juice and wine so had some Vitamin C. She suspected it was the healthiest drink Michaels had in a long time.

"Starving party of two," the hostess announced over the loudspeaker.

"That's us," Michaels said, and he grabbed a drink in each hand.

Crystal chandeliers dripped from the ceiling of the Terrace Room. Floor-to-ceiling windows displayed a panoramic view of Central Park where vibrant colors of trees flashed a kaleidoscope of fall colors. Inside, spring bloomed. Bouquets of flowers seemed to grow from the Terrace Room floor, sprouting from the center of the tables. Even the tablecloths grew fields of pink roses. The dining room smelled of old-lady perfumes, dripping with rose nectar.

"The eggs Benedict are a classic," Michaels said, ordering what amounted to a loaf of toast with his dozen scrambled eggs.

"You sure are hungry," she said.

He grinned sheepishly. "I haven't eaten since the hot dogs you bought me."

Right, he normally drinks his meals.

She sipped on her second glass of wine, eyeing him above the rim of her glass. "What was Jake like?"

"Your brother was a dumb ass."

She slammed her glass down. "I thought you were Jake's friend yet you speak ill of him, even though he's…dead."

Michaels grabbed her wrist and squeezed.

"Ouch. You're going to break my bones," she said.

"You've misunderstood." He loosened his pressure, but his fingers still dug into her arm.

"You're hurting me."

"Sorry." He pushed her arm away.

She rubbed her chafed skin.

"I don't want to hurt you, Mandy. I really don't."

The regret in his voice disturbed her, as if it was a given that he would hurt her. The longer they looked into each other's eyes, the more flustered Michaels became.

He guzzled a glass of champagne and then cleared his throat. "What I meant to say was that your brother could have saved himself but chose to stay behind to help an injured man. The guy was a stranger, trapped by fallen debris. He was a selfish man who should have told Jacob to think of himself and get the hell out of the building. Now me, I would have left the man to die, but no, your brother had to be noble. Jacob is the bravest man I ever knew, but a real dumb ass," he said, and slammed his empty glass on the table, shattering the stem. "Bring me a glass of whiskey," he said to the waitress who was cleaning the broken glass from the tablecloth.

"Exactly what happened that morning?" Miranda braced herself to hear about Jake's death.

"That's all there is. No more. End of story," he said, flatly.

Funny, she never noticed the gashes in his hands before. His cuts were not fresh from the glass he just broke. *Maybe his wound is from 9/11,* she thought.

He emptied a glass into a water pitcher and then poured wine from the bottle into the glass.

She stirred her eggs Benedict, turning the classic into scrambled eggs.

Neither spoke for the duration of their meal.

He ate only one slice of toast, crumbling the rest into bite-size pieces, and filling up a doggy bag.

"A snack?" she said.

"A meal," he replied.

Holy shit, this restaurant is expensive, she thought, eyeing the check. "It's a good thing I have two credit cards." she said, gritting her teeth.

He didn't offer to split the check. Michaels seemed content to let her pay.

They left Tavern on the Green, and he swung the doggy bag.

Ashes darted from under the bunny shrub, following them with his tail wagging. They crossed through a crowd traveling on roller blades and bicycles. Early fallen leaves crunched beneath their shoes as they headed southeasterly. Ashes ran ahead, sniffing the ground, and stopping now and then to lift his leg.

She cocked her head to carnival-like music coming from an opening in the trees. "It's the carousel."

"Yup," he said, walking in the opposite direction.

"But I love carousel rides." Miranda yanked him towards the music.

"There will be a line," he warned.

"I'm used to waiting," she said with a gleam in her eyes.

Michaels snorted at her barb.

"The carousel is so big." She marveled at the almost life-size horses around the outer ring, some rearing their hind legs and others with legs in mid-stride. The rafters beneath the canopy were painted red, and red ribbons of trim encircled the canopy with brightly colored pictures painted in between the ribbons.

"Fifty-eight horses," he said while they stood in line.

"You counted?"

"When I was a kid. The carousel is a 1908 Stein and Goldstein abandoned in the trolley terminal on Coney Island."

"It's magnificent," she said, eyeing her horse. Miranda jumped on the platform and made her way over. She climbed on a green saddle, patting the hand-carved horse on its neck. She rubbed the horse across its blonde mane, whispering into its ear, "You're a beauty, though a bit wild looking, like Michaels."

Its mouth was wide open, looking as if the horse was traveling at breakneck speed. In fact, the horse appeared as if the devil chased it, kind of like Michaels.

He never took his eyes off her as the carousel circled.

Wind-swept, she stepped off the carousel and into his outstretched arms.

"What did you say to the horse?" he said.

"I told the horse to trust me," she said, looking him in the eye.

He jerked her arms from around his neck and stormed off.

She followed him to the east side of the park, close to Fifth Avenue. His silence grated on her nerves but damned if she would speak first.

Miniature boats raced around a green pond where a group of kids were gathered.

Michaels cheered for a Chinese Junk.

Miranda cheered for a sleek schooner.

He gave her a triumphant smirk when the Chinese Junk won.

"You obviously know how to pick them," she said, biting her lip for being the first to break their silence.

"The water will ice up by December in the boat pond." He pointed to a large hill nearby. "I used to sled down Pilgrim's Hill when I was a kid. There's nothing like skating on the ice in Central Park," he said nostalgically.

"I've only ever lived where it's too warm for ice skates."

"When do you go back to Los Angeles?"

"I have just three days to find out about Jake. Have you ever been to California?"

"Nope."

"You should some time. It's lovely. If you ever come to Los Angeles, I could return the favor and show you around."

An uncomfortable silence hung between them.

§

Chapter 22:1

Now there is in Manhattan
By the Sheep Meadow
A fountain called Bethesda.
Therein lay a great multitude of sick people
Waiting for the moving of the water.

Michaels picked up a penny from the ground and bounced it on her shoe. "Here's a coin for the fountain at Bethesda Terrace where you can make a wish for your true love to sweep you off your feet."

She picked up the rusted penny.

"That coin won't even buy a piece of bubble gum," he said, "which is about what love is worth. People chew on love, blowing bubbles until the gum loses its flavor, and then the bubble bursts, splattering their faces with sticky residue."

Nevertheless, she clenched the penny.

They wandered south to Bethesda Terrace, mingling with a crowd on the red brick.

Michaels pointed to a lush green field "The Sheep Meadow where sheep grazed in the 1800's."

"How odd to think of Manhattan as having ever been anything but what it is now," she said.

"Well the city has changed since 9/11."

A makeshift minister stood near a fountain. He quoted in a booming voice, "Gospel of St. John. Chapter five. Verses two through four. Now there is in Jerusalem by the Sheep Gate a pool which is called in Hebrew Bethesda, having five porches. In these lay a multitude of sick people, blind, lame, paralyzed, waiting for the moving water."

Like the Biblical Bethesda, the city's Bethesda was surrounded by the sick. Their sickness was of the human heart.

The hippy-looking, holy man rolled up his pants and climbed into the fountain. "I am the voice of one calling in Central Park. Prepare for the way of the Lord."

The crowd formed a line in order to be baptized in water splashing from a statue of a winged angel, which was the fountain centerpiece.

The holy man held up a hand. "There before me came a pale horse. Its rider was named Al-Qaeda, and Hades was following close behind him."

Miranda refused to pollute Bethesda fountain by throwing a penny in for a selfish wish. There should be doves circling, but only hungry pigeons flew over the area.

Michaels scattered his breakfast toast around the bricks. Pigeons flocked around him.

"That's all there is," he told the birds, shaking his doggy bag upside down.

He pointed straight across from Bethesda Terrace towards Fifth Avenue. "That's where I grew up. My parents live there still," he said, staring longingly at the building.

"Do you have any brothers and sisters?"

"My sister Rebecca. And Lyle, a brother."

"What does your brother do?"

"He's an obstetrician, but I'd rather not talk about Lyle," he said, frowning.

Nor my brother either, she thought, fuming.

"Come on. I want you to see my dog," he said, motioning for her to follow.

Near the children's zoo, he patted the bronze rump of the statue of a dog. Proud and faithful, with its tongue sticking out, the dog appeared to be panting with a dogsled harness strapped to its back.

"Balto could not be your dog," she said, reading the sign. "In 1925, this Siberian Husky was the lead dog of a dogsled team that braved an Alaskan blizzard some 660 miles to deliver a serum to stop a diphtheria epidemic in Nome."

"Well, he looks like my dog, and my husky is named Balto. His tail curls just like this," he said, flipping his hand like the tail of the statue. "I used to walk my Balto on crisp fall afternoons like today and stop for an Espresso, strong and hot, just like my city," he said in a voice filled with sadness.

Perhaps his Balto was dead, like the heroic Balto who survived his hazardous journey. Balto came to Manhattan for the dedication of his statue but died a short time later.

"Did Jake have any pets?"

He looked at Ashes and frowned.

Ashes hung his head, staring at the sidewalk.

"Jake was crazy about our dog when we were kids," she said. "I don't know what happened to Spotty, but I still remember Jake screaming when the animal shelter took him away, right before we were sent to separate foster homes. Jake cried for Spotty, and I cried for Jake. Spotty was Jake's dog." She patted the bronze Balto. "Did Jake ever mention a dog? Did you ever go to his apartment and see a pet? Did he have a picture on his desk at work? Of a girl? Of a dog?"

"Or a girl who is a dog?"

"Very funny. Answer my question."

"Which question? Balto!" he said in a shocked voice.

She swung her head to the direction of a fierce growl.

"Come on, boy, it's me," he said, holding out his hand to a Siberian husky. Like the Balto statue, this dog stood with its legs wide apart but did not have a gentle look on its furry face. The fur on its back stood straight up.

Michaels snapped his fingers at the dog and whistled.

The dog bared its teeth and snapped.

"Are you sure that's your dog?" she whispered, taking a step back.

"First off, his collar is a Harley-Davidson dog collar. Secondly, the dog has white paws, and his back paw has black spots. I wonder who's walking him." Michaels surveyed the area with a cautious look, like he was ready to bolt.

§

Chapter 23:1

And so a new era is written in the ashes of stone,
Before 9/11 and After 9/11.

Ashes came running up the path.

The fierce husky Michaels claimed was his dog whined, and ran with its tail tucked between its legs, its leash flying in the wind.

Miranda laughed at the big husky running away from small Ashes, like the devil chased it. "Your bully dog is scared of Ashes. Go figure."

"Balto will be alright," Michaels said in a voice still insisting the dog was his.

"Perhaps your dog has amnesia too."

"Balto? I think my dog is fine, just upset over..."

"Jealousy of your love for a bronze dog? Is that why your dog acted as if he would like to tear your throat open?"

"Don't exaggerate."

An older man came running up the path. He was a bit winded. "Balto," he yelled.

Michaels ducked behind Balto's statue.

The man ran past them. "Balto," he kept hollering.

Miranda stepped behind the statue where Michaels knelt rubbing his forehead. She had no idea if he had a headache, but his large hand hid his face from anyone passing by.

"You were right. The dog's name is Balto. That man looking for your dog, who was he," she said.

"I just thought it was my dog." He wiped a tear from his eye.

"Maybe you should see a therapist, Dr. Michaels."

"I don't need that kind of help. There is nothing wrong with my mind," he snapped. He punched his forehead.

"Well you're not much use to me with only half a memory."

"Right," he said, scanning her body and focusing his eyes on her breasts. "Brunettes have never been my type, Lady. Nor have I ever liked bad-tempered women. What the hell am I doing with you anyway?" he spat and spun on his heel.

With a forlorn look, she stared at his back. Michaels was walking fast.

I'm such a bitch, she thought, her boots crunching the leaves.

His back was hunched over and his hands buried in his pockets. Michaels walked with his head down. He appeared shrunken. She hurried to catch up with him, but Michaels turned a corner and vanished into the foliage of Central Park as mysteriously as he appeared at her hotel this morning.

She stumbled down the path. "Michaels," she yelled, circling and looking for any sign of him. It was easy to hide in Central Park.

It's over. I'll never see him again. Miranda pulled at her hair, groaning, "Well, Jake, I've done it again. Today, I've lost a friend. Well not exactly my friend—your friend. I've put my foot in it."

I should never have let Michaels kiss me yesterday. This isn't an out-of-town fling. It's for the best I don't see him again.

But what of Jake, her heart whispered.

Michaels had said that maybe, there is a ghost between us. Your brother has thrown us together. Do you really think it's a coincidence, that out of all the thousands mourning at Ground Zero, it happened to be me you bumped into?

"Well, I hope you are wrong, Michaels, else I've let down my brother too," she said and headed back to her hotel.

Ashes followed with a hangdog look.

§

Chapter 24:1

And candles will flicker and burn,
Their Lights extinguished too soon,
And lives melting away with the summer.

With a feeling of déjà vu, Miranda returned to Central Park at the stroke of midnight. She flickered on the fringes of a candlelight vigil. It was dark in the back where she hid. She cowered before a tall tree.

Children, who should have been tucked in bed, sat on the shoulders of relatives and waved American flags.

The crowd was of like mind, humming the tune of a funeral march. The mourners each held a single candle. Candlelight shone beneath their faces, making them appear like zombies. The scene was reminiscent of a horror film that took place at a cemetery—*Night of the Living Dead.*

Whoosh.

Someone blew out her candle. Miranda gagged from the stench of a cigar. Goosebumps erupted on her skin.

Someone breathed down her neck.

A deep voice whispered into her ear obscene words.

She pushed her hand into her purse, shoveling through the contents. *The Mace? Where's the Mace?*

Hairs rubbed across her palm.

A hand inside my purse—a big hand!

She screamed and a hand slapped across her mouth

Oh, my God! Oh, my God! I can't breathe.

Quit panicking! Think. Think.

Where's my cell phone!?

She stomped her foot down.

Her purse swung loosely from her shoulder.

Miranda pulled out a lighter and with shaky fingers, relit her candle.

She held the candle up and was startled by Michaels. His features appeared sinister and spooky, illuminated by the light of the candle. His eyes especially looked odd, haunted, and hollow yet filled with—remorse?

"Is everything okay?" he said.

§

Chapter 25:1

And the mayor will stumble and fall.

Michaels reached out a hand to her. I'm so sorry for you, his eyes seemed to say.

"Did you…," she said, "were you just…" Now what? Miranda couldn't tell Michaels a man shoved his hand in her purse because she practically accused him.

His soft look melted her eyes to boiling chocolate. His own eyes lightened to a silvery gray.

She entwined her hand with his, squeezing his fingers. *God help me, I don't know whether to trust this man. Michaels might have been trying to steal my wallet. He never has any money of his own.*

Miranda did not question how he happened to find her in this sorry crowd in the dead of night, under a moonless night glittering with candles. Suddenly, the world didn't seem so dark.

His hand was warm and tingly. Electricity shot up her arm.

The ball of his thumb rubbed her palm like he made love to her.

Her hand trembled.

His eyes turned a smoky gray, desire swirling around his pupils.

Miranda blushed and lowered her eyes. She snatched her hand from his and took a deep breath. *Control. Control.*

But all she could think of was Michaels and running into the woods with him. The dark night would cloak them. The grass would be soft against her back.

She inhaled the sweetness of grass, a clean, fresh smell of nature seducing the senses until a woman can't think of anything but the tug of grass beneath her fingers, the pull of a man's silken hair, and the feel of his muscular back.

"It's cold tonight," she said in a breathless voice.

Real original. It's cold tonight. Duh. Let's talk about something neutral like the weather instead of what I really meant—that the grass would be cold, but you would warm me. Miranda swallowed. *Behave yourself.* She balled her hands, digging her nails into her skin.

"I know you didn't mean to be so callous earlier," he said.

"Don't be so sure. You know little about me. I can be a real bitch when the movement hits me. Just like that." She snapped her fingers. "I'm moody and temperamental. No one wanted to adopt me or even keep me as a foster child. I was kicked out of a dozen families. Social Services have a file on me as long as your arm." *You forgot to mention the Juvenile Detention Home and slut with your resume. With Michaels it would be more than sex*—this thought frightened her the most because for Michaels, it would not be the same, *if I lay with him, here, on the grass. Only with him.*

"I know you're sweet and you're warm and you loved your brother a great deal," he said.

"Don't make me sound like an angel or make excuses for me. I was a little girl who grew into a selfish woman who only thinks of herself," she said, her voice cracking.

"Being separated from your brother must have been hard. My city brings the hurt back to you." He sounded full of remorse as if her problems were his fault, his and Manhattan's. He added, "I overreacted earlier. Since 9/11 I've become too sensitive and emotional. I'm impatient and moved to anger."

"I should have been more understanding of what happened to you. Asking you to relive bad memories is not fair to you, Michaels."

"Call me Christopher."

Too personal.

"Mandy, coming all the way to look for your brother is not the act of a selfish woman. I can't believe you could have done anything to warrant such guilt. If you didn't love Jacob so much, you wouldn't be here with me, a stranger." He looked suspiciously around the darkened area.

"Boo. Expecting an ambush are we?" she said, grinning.

"It's late. Anywhere people are there is danger."

"Whew. What made you so mistrustful?" she said.

"I never trust a stranger."

"But I'm a stranger."

"Ah, but I knew your brother. Jacob is the tie that binds us." He leaned into her and winked. "You'll just have to trust me."

"My mother taught me never to trust strangers," she said lightly.

"Don't worry, Mandy, I've yet to offer you any candy."

"I don't think I want your candy." She crossed her fingers behind her back. *Liar. Liar. Pants on fire.*

"No? Well, here we are a man and a woman."

And the woods behind us. A bed of grass, a roof of sky, and let nature take its course.

He ran a finger down her nose.

"Don't," she said.

"Don't?"

She sighed with frustration. He of all people should want the distance between them. Don't touch me—he had said. Well he threw down the gauntlet. "We're not on a date, Michaels that winds up with us in bed and you tiptoeing from my room before breakfast and screaming that relationships make you claustrophobic and make your head hurt."

"I know. We have to play this thing out to the end."

"This thing?"

"You and I, Mandy. Fate has somehow thrown us together."

"Fate? I thought you said it was Jake who threw us together."

"What did you do after I left you?" he said, smiling.

I missed you. I thought I would never see you again, and I hate you for making me miss you. I dislike you for not telling me about Jake. But all she confessed was, “I went to Yankee Stadium.”

“Ah. A baseball game. I'm a rabid Yankees fan,” he said in a voice filled with yearning.

“As I sat in the House that Ruth built I pictured Jake at the ballgame. Was my brother a Yankees fan?”

He shrugged his shoulders.

“As a kid, Jake was nuts for sports,” she said. “I imagined him sitting beside me eating a hot dog. You know what I saw?”

He reached out his hand and stroked her cheek, just the lightest touch across her scar, like a feather. “What did you see?” he gently said.

“The Mayor of New York City looking like walking death from lack of sleep. He seemed to carry the city's burdens upon his shoulders, its grief and fears, a sinking economy and hopes for a bright future. A prayer service was being held. There were men in uniform, firemen and policemen, grieving for their missing comrades. The dead were there too, not just their photographs. I could feel their presence. For a moment, it really did seem as if Jake sat beside me. What got to me was the mayor, that seemingly unbreakable pillar the nation has leaned upon since 9/11, completely losing it.”

Her candle burned out, engulfing them in darkness.

His breathing was labored and his body heat scorching. He would think her a slut if she pulled him down to the grass and frolicked in the woods, nude, beside him. Michaels said he fell in love every time he walked into a bar. If Miranda had not met him at Ground Zero, she might have met him at a bar and followed him home, just like his other one-night stands, and there must have been many. Did Michaels respect any of the ladies in the morning, or laugh at them for giving in so easily? Did he mock them for leaving his apartment with stomachs yearning for breakfast and a man to share food with for a lifetime?

"My candle's burned out. I have to go now," she said, handing the wick to Michaels.

They stood under a street lamp, and he stared at her perplexed.

Miranda walked hurriedly away. She wasn't far from the Eighty-Sixth Street Transverse Road.

The driver of a white carriage and feathered horse tipped his top hat to her.

"Up you go," Michaels said, grabbing her elbow and dragging her over to the carriage.

She had heard no footsteps behind her. "Where did you come from?" she said.

§

Chapter 26:1

Laughter and play will slowly return.

"I was right behind you the whole time," Michaels said.

"No, you weren't. I would have heard you."

"I tread lightly," he said with double meaning, like Michaels warned her that he was careful with women and easily scared off.

He helped her into the carriage.

She was too easy and too compliant. With Michaels, she was more than willing to follow his command. Miranda melted like butter on the carriage seat.

"I've always wanted to take a carriage ride through Central Park," he said, jumping up beside her on the red leather seat.

Ashes sat across from them, watching, with a strange expression in his doggy eyes.

"Your chaperone?" Michaels said.

"It's a bit chilly for an outdoor ride," she said.

"The driver has the top up. Sort of Victorian, don't you think? Let's see. How does the poem go? How do I love thee? Let me count the ways."

She snorted at his dancing eyes that belied his words of devotion in quoting the Elizabeth Browning poem. Miranda was shocked he could quote the beginning verbatim.

He leaned closer to her. "How do I love thee? Let me count the ways. I love you for your temper. Your bitchiness. Moodiness. Mysteriousness. And clumsiness. And if this shall be my last breath, I will love you even more after death."

Michaels could not mean any of his poetry. Of course, he did not love her. "You got the first two sentences right. The poem ends: and, if God choose, I shall but love thee better after death," she said coolly.

"What the hell if I stole some of Browning's words? You're turning me into a poet, Mandy. Here we are taking a romantic carriage ride. Before the night is over, your conversion of me may be complete."

"Me converting you?"

"You're turning me into a soap-opera romantic." He sighed deeply, placing a hand over his heart.

"So, did Jake root for the Yankees?"

"Doesn't every New Yorker?"

"The stadium was decorated with black ribbons and wreathes."

"Can we forget about death for awhile?" he said wearily.

The horse clip-clopped at a leisurely pace, traversing the lit pathways of Central Park, paths the horse probably could have walked with blinders on.

Miranda shivered, buttoning her jacket to her neck. She clucked her tongue at his short sleeves. "You're going to catch pneumonia. You look flushed. Are you feverish?"

"A little," he said, yawning

"Feel okay?"

"Yeah."

She placed a palm on his forehead. His skin felt cool.

"No one has mothered me in a long time," he drawled.

He locked his fingers around her wrist and dragged her hand from his forehead down to his crotch.

"Don't," she said.

"Liar," he said and lowered his mouth to her palm. He licked her wrist, sucking on her large vein.

Her pulse danced wildly with his tongue. She swallowed, fighting the urge to stroke his hair.

He rolled his chin around her palm and raised his eyes to her face.

She jerked her hand back and his chin almost fell to the floor.

He leaned against the seat, chuckling.

She breathed heavily.

"Hot are we?" he said, placing a hand across her forehead and grinning.

She slapped his hand away. "What's this we business? Why are you referring to me as we?"

"You started it when you said, 'expecting an ambush are we?' Want us to be a couple?" he said, wiggling his eyebrows.

"Oh, shut up!"

"If you're worried about me catching cold, a kiss would warm me," he said, smiling lazily.

"Where exactly would a kiss lead? I can just see you the morning after." She mimicked his deep voice, "I didn't mean for that to happen, but it seemed the right thing to do since I was bare ass naked. Now I'm feeling remorseful."

He pecked at her cheek.

Her heart plummeted. "I suppose you've always wanted another sister," she said.

"You? Not likely. You're too contrary. You say no and then complain. Just like a woman to say no when she means yes. And what about you? Looking for a big brother, Mandy?"

"I had a brother, remember? I came to New York to find Jake. No one can ever replace him."

"I haven't forgotten why you're with me," he said, sighing up at the carriage ceiling. "How about a father then?"

"You're too young to be my father, thank you very much. What are you, six years older than me?"

"Seven. I'm seven years older."

They spent the rest of their carriage ride bantering lightly, neither winning nor willing to give an inch.

The driver left them in front of the Plaza Hotel and for once Michaels paid.

The street was lined with empty carriages. Forgotten dreams. Lost moments.

Michaels looked over at the modern carriage, the taxi cab awaiting her, and then down at his shoes. "Well, sweet dreams, Mandy," he said and walked away. Once more, his shoulders were rounded and he appeared shrunken.

Just climb in the cab. Don't you dare ask him to come back to the hotel with you!

"Good night, Michaels," she whispered, slamming the cab door. He acted gentle tonight. She preferred him as an asshole.

You're playing with fire, a voice whispered in her head.

"Well here's to fire," she murmured.

On the way back to the Algonquin with Ashes sleeping in her lap, all Miranda could think about were lost moments.

Unspoken words.

Withheld invitations.

How could the day have fallen through the cracks of time? Time is an oak with leaves falling, she thought.

Miranda suddenly longed for home, her own bed, and her safe world of last week that didn't include Michaels or ghosts.

There exists only this moment. Now. A lifetime.

Lost moments, her life was filled with lost moments.

Miranda wrinkled her brow. Michaels had paid for the carriage ride. There had been that hand in her purse and then Michaels showing up right afterwards. And for once, he had money to pay.

She opened her purse and counted her cash. Damn! Miranda couldn't remember how much she had.

§

Chapter 27:1

And tape will be erected
To block the face of terror.

Monday, September 24, 2001

There was a misty sheen at Ground Zero. Miranda stood in thick fog swirling around the yellow tape. A voice echoed through the fog above, below, and right through her. *Mandy,* the voice whispered.

The voice was familiar and the tone so haunting. *Mandy.*

"Jake?" she said, blinking at the fog merging into human form. *He's finally come. Jake knows I haven't much time left in New York,* she thought, remembering his childhood promise—I'll come back. Somehow, some way, I shall contact you.

Her heart beat with excitement at a dark blot in the fog taking shape and resembling the shadow of a man.

The shadow floated with awkwardness, seeming shy and unsure of his welcome.

Miranda stood with open arms. She had waited thirteen years. At last. Now. This moment. A lifetime. Jake.

The odor of a bank vault snaked through her nostrils. The stench of money drifted to her nose, smelling like the rusted copper of a penny and a dollar clenched in sweaty palms.

Fog swirled above her, slowly evaporating to reveal hunched shoulders, overcoat, and galoshes. The stench of money was replaced by the stink of stale beer and wine. The face took the form of Michaels, waffling in the fog and unsteady on his feet from drink.

"Mandy, it's only me," he said in a sad tone. "Are you ready?"

She did not question his waiting for her at Ground Zero. Fate somehow threw them together. Miranda was beginning to trust fate. Michaels would tell her about Jake.

In this fog she could lose Michaels, so she clasped his hand.

They walked, their shoes splashing against the sidewalk the only sound until footsteps crept behind them.

She glanced over her shoulder, unable to tell who followed in the fog. *Jake,* she thought.

A burly man stepped into the light of a street lamp.

"You got a problem, Mister?" Michaels yelled in his face, poking a finger in his chest.

The man threw up his hands, showing he was unarmed. He took off running down the street.

Michaels was no longer the joking man from the wee hours of the morning who bantered with her, joked and laughed in the carriage. He seemed balanced on the edge of a cliff. His eyes were more bloodshot, his face fatigued. He appeared to not have slept in a long time.

"Are you okay?" she said.

He grunted, sounding too weak for the niceties of polite conversation, safe conversation, and how-the-hell's-the-weather today conversation.

"Have you eaten," she said.

"Not since yesterday morning," he admitted.

"Tavern on the Green?"

He nodded.

She linked her arm through his, wondering if Michaels had been evicted from the apartment he claimed to live in. Had he always been so down on his luck, or did 9/11 affect him so much? He seemed to be lost, suffering from post traumatic stress besides a head injury. "There has got to be a restaurant nearby. In Manhattan we're never far from food. Come on, I'll buy you a meal," she said.

"I'd rather not stay in this area," he said and looked around like something or someone was going to snatch him.

"We'll take a cab then," she said.

"Nope. Subway."

"Subway?" she screeched.

He dragged her to the Chambers Street Station.

A cab would have been the better choice, given the recent terrorist attacks. The subway station was crowded. Miranda bought two tokens from a vending machine, and they sprinted down the steps to the trains. Michaels stumbled on the last two, losing his balance and nearly falling.

"Maybe you shouldn't drink so much," she murmured.

He gave her a dirty look and spit on the walkway.

The subway walls were lined with graffiti, and the air was stale.

A train sped across the tracks, rustling up the air, and blowing the stink of the subway bowels into her nostrils. Her stomach twisted, wanting to chug up her breakfast. The heat the train generated made Miranda feel faint, reminding her of her nightmare that first night after she saw Jake's ghost.

A train screeched to a halt, and the doors slid open, some passengers departing. Miranda and Michaels walked through the opening.

He sauntered over to the corner and sat, munching on a candy bar she bought him.

Miranda plopped down next to him, Ashes sitting beneath her feet.

Michaels peeled off his raincoat, placing it on the other side. He removed his galoshes, hiding them underneath the seat. Michaels loosened his wrinkled tie and rolled up his sleeves. He leaned back, linking his fingers across his flat stomach.

His head bounced in rhythm with the train.

With bold eyes she studied the sleeping Michaels. He was paler today, probably from not having eaten. Muscles bulged from his forearms that had a sprinkling of light hair. He wore no watch. His right fist, where he had punched the wall, was unmarked. He had no bruises or redness. There was no cracked skin or swelling. There was no sign he ever punched a concrete wall day before yesterday.

Well, he was wearing gloves, she thought.

Michaels wore no wedding band.

His lashes were dark, long and thick. His face was unblemished like he'd never had a pimple in his life. Michaels was clean-shaven for once, and it was obvious he had to shave daily. His cheekbones were high and strong. He had a square jaw and wide, smooth lips.

A couple of open shirt buttons exposed his chest and some golden-brown hair.

She moved her eyes down lower to his battered belt buckle.

Down further.

Further.

There.

Michaels coughed and she blushed. Miranda had been staring, thinking he was sleeping.

He dropped his eyes to her legs, ogling her like she had him. His eyes rose to her skirt, stopping at the V joining her legs.

She wanted to smack him in the face. Instead, she snapped her fingers.

He raised an eyebrow. "You're too skinny, too California, and too needy. Your virginity is safe from me," he drawled even as he looked at her like a rapist.

She lifted her chin and said, "I am not a virgin."

He grinned, wiggling his eyebrows.

Just chop my tongue to pieces! My damn pride has made a fool of me again. Miranda had wanted him to know that even though she wasn't his type, there were plenty of men who preferred her. She could kick herself in the teeth. She did not wish to play games with him and suspected that if she ever did, she would be the one to get burned.

Michaels already scorched you, inside and out. Run home like a hurt little girl. Take a cold shower.

"I'm not here to discuss my sex life," she hissed, too late.

His smug smile boasted he didn't wish to talk about sex either. He just wanted to get on with it.

"If this is where this conversation is heading," she said.

"You can't exactly get off the train, can you?"

"No, but I don't have to sit here with you," she said and stood.

"Chill out, Mandy, where's your sense of humor?"

The look in his eyes chastened her, and she sat back down. Michaels had a gift for making the other person feel guilty. In all fairness, she started this. He caught her gawking and at least was gentleman enough not to mention it. On the other hand, he had stared at her in such a nasty way.

As if you didn't. As if you're not as guilty as he.

"Am I your type?" he said.

"I don't like blondes," she said and was not in a talking mood for the rest of their short trip.

The subway chugged along, snaking its way beneath Manhattan.

"Wherever are we going?" she said when they climbed the subway steps and into the light.

"Chinatown."

"More hot dogs? We could have found a hot dog vendor without taking the subway."

"No hot dogs. Been there. Done that."

"Nuts?" she said, pointing her chin to the vendor he purchased nuts from the other day.

"Done that too."

"Italian or Chinese then?" she said. Little Italy was down the street from Chinatown.

Michaels grabbed her elbow, steering her through Little China. Banners of Chinese symbols waved in the wind. Ducks swung in windows lined with fortune cookies. Statues of smiling Buddhas stared from shop windows. There were many Chinese restaurants to choose from.

"The Four Joys is my favorite," he said.

The hostess bowed and shuffled them over to a corner, black shellac table.

They sat beneath hanging paper lanterns. The placemats had the twelve years of the Chinese calendar drawn around with an animal symbol for each year. The fish tank across from them had a striped fish resembling a tiger—the Chinese year she was born in.

The last Year of the Tiger was 1998. Miranda tried to remember if 1998 had been a good year. It had. She completed four years of a Bachelor's degree in just two years and began teaching. The next Year of the Tiger would be 2010. A long time to wait for another good year.

"Let's see," she said, circling the calendar with her finger until she found the right animal. She scratched at its whiskers. "I suppose you were born in the Year of the Rat," she murmured.

"Very funny. You must have been born in the year of the Ox because you are so damned stubborn."

"And you were born in the Year of the Pig, which is really the Year of the Boar."

He laughed, lifting a glass of water to his lips.

"Did Jake like Chinese food?" she said.

"How the heck would I know what Jake liked to eat? I don't pay attention to what everyone else eats. Just my own stomach."

Strike three. So Michaels and Jake had not eaten at a Chinese restaurant together. Miranda was getting awfully tired of his "how the heck would I know" excuse. "Did you eat at any other restaurants with my brother?"

"What's your horoscope sign?"

"Virgo."

"The virgin," he said with dancing eyes.

"And your sign?"

"Gemini."

The twins. Figures. Michaels is two men. She picked up her chopsticks, stabbing them into her rice. Grains flew across the table, striking him.

He wiped his face with his napkin. "Attacking me with rice in public? You've wounded me, Mandy. You are dangerous with those chopsticks," he said, grinning.

A Chinese man wearing glasses as thick as bottles shuffled up to their table. A camera dangled around his neck. "Picture only ten dollar," he said, bowing.

Michaels narrowed his eyes at her. "Okay," he said.

"Wait." She wiped a flake of rice from his lips.

He grabbed her shoulder, pulling their heads together. "Smile for the camera," he said.

The camera clicked, the flash blinding her.

"Here. You keep it." Michaels threw the picture at her.

"Thanks," she murmured. In the picture she resembled a fool, staring at Michaels with a dumbstruck expression, like she was beginning to believe in fairy tales, and that somewhere out there happiness did exist. She dropped the picture into her purse, snapping it shut.

They cracked open their fortune cookies.

"Oh look. I have two fortunes in one cookie," she said excitedly. She read aloud, "You will hear from someone you have not seen in a long time." She folded the piece of paper and cocked her head. "In a way, this has already come true—I will hear from Jake through you. Like you said, fate and Jake have somehow thrown us together."

His response sounded more like a grunt than a yes.

Miranda read her other fortune. "All is not always what it seems." She balled her fortunes into trash, dropping the paper in her purse. She folded her hands, resting her chin on her fingers. "Your turn," she said.

Michaels held his fortune up to the light and read to himself. He crumpled the fortune, throwing it on his empty plate.

At the door Miranda said, "Shoot, I forgot to leave the tip. You go ahead and I'll catch up," she said, opening her purse.

Michaels waited outside the restaurant.

Miranda hurried back to the table, left four bills, and grabbed his fortune from his plate.

She straightened the wrinkled piece of paper and read: He who manipulates fate gets what he deserves.

§

Chapter 28:1

And the little animals will suffer.

"It's not a sin to enjoy yourself while you're here, Mandy. What would you like to do this afternoon? You'll only be here a few more days. You may never come back," Michaels said, as if he already missed her, as though he couldn't bear to part from her.

No. No. I must be mistaken.

"Am I keeping you from something?" she said, *or someone* she thought.

"Nope. Where to?"

"I've already taken too much of your time."

"Time has no meaning."

"No?"

"Not anymore. Not today. Not while I'm with you." He winked at her. "Where to? Your wish is my command, my Lady," he said, his eyes brightening to silver. He stroked her lips with his index finger. "Sh. I've got time. I want to do this. I need to do this."

Her lips tingled from the touch of his finger. Her stomach moved, or was it the earth rumbling, threatening to swallow her? *Oh God. What's happening to me? What's he thinking?*

"Well? What do you want, Mandy?" he said in a husky voice pulling her towards him, making her want more than she would dare.

Miranda clenched her fists, fighting her attraction to him. "I want you to tell me about Jake," she said.

"Not now! Why are you trying to ruin everything?" His eyes appeared tortured.

Jesus, he has a way of making me feel guilty. Why does Michaels have to look at me like a hurt little boy? Why couldn't I be flippant and sophisticated, toss my hair and coolly say, what do you want, Michaels? She lowered her eyes. *What am I thinking of? Miranda, get a grip on yourself.*

"Sure I'm not keeping you?" she said.

"Nope. I have no place to go," he said, shrugging his broad shoulders.

Me neither. Not anymore. Now that Jake is gone, I can never really go home again. Ever, she thought, but hesitated asking him about Jake again, else he might storm off like a spoiled child. Later, he said, later. She would drag information out of him. Maybe if she got him drunk…

"There is only one touristy thing I would like to do—Ellis Island. You are lucky to have family, Michaels. I only had Jake left, and he's been taken from me. I still remember our mother telling us that our Great-Grandfather came to California in 1898 from Spain through Ellis Island," she said.

"Ghosts again huh? Ellis Island is filled with ghosts of immigrants who died there from disease or plain bad luck. Some could only dream of freedom from their one glimpse of the Statue of Liberty as they arrived at port and then wondered, after being detained for weeks, if they would ever be let off the island to experience that liberty. Ellis Island has a spooky feel when you walk the deserted rooms once lined with immigrants who were penned in. Before benches were provided, they had to stand in lines for days to be processed. In its heyday, Ellis Island was known as, Island of Tears, Island of Hope, but you're out of luck today, Mandy, because hope is closed to all visitors since 9/11."

"That's too bad. What of your roots?"

"Irish all the way. My Great-Great-Great-Grandfather Michaels made his way to Liverpool, England, boarded an ocean liner and never looked back to starving Ireland, County Cork."

"Well, since Ellis Island is closed, I would like to go shopping at Macy's."

Michaels snapped open the boxes of left-over Chinese food, setting them on the sidewalk. "Dig in," he told Ashes.

"You are going to make the dog sick."

"Nah. Chinese food is his favorite isn't it, Boy?" he said, scratching the dog's head.

Ashes wagged his tail.

"His favorite? How do you know that?"

"The dog told me so. Just wish I'd brought him some chopsticks."

She sighed down at the little dog licking the boxes clean.

"Why the long face?" he said.

"I don't know what I'm going to do with Ashes. No one has answered the advertisement."

"Well, I wouldn't fret over him if I was you."

Miranda waited for Michaels to offer to take Ashes, but he could barely take care of himself, much less a dog. She gave a heartfelt sigh. "Guess I'll have to turn him over to the Animal Control Center, which I should have done when I found him at Ground Zero. There was a cat huddling on the roof of a WTC building. The cat was apparently a survivor, scorched but none the worse for wear. A family from out West adopted the cat. Now I'm afraid the authorities won't believe me when I tell them where I found Ashes."

He cleared his throat. "Some of the offices of the Twin Towers allowed employees to take their pets to work."

"You think maybe Ashes…"

Michaels played with his earlobe so she suspected he was nervous about something. "I think I've said too much. I shouldn't speculate," he said.

"Well, we can't prove Ashes is a survivor. Who knows how the dog ended up at Ground Zero or how long he was there. I'm afraid for the little guy, in case no one wants him. I would adopt him, but I have a cat that freaks out if a dog even comes into the yard. Whiskey likes to sit on the window sill and look out at his world. Ashes would drive Whiskey to an early grave."

"Don't get so attached to the dog. Ashes will be okay won't you, Boy?"

Ashes barked, licking his chops.

"Maybe you can keep him," she suggested.

Again, he didn't offer.

"Oh, I forgot about your dog, Balto, who doesn't seem to know who you are."

"I repeat—don't worry about Ashes," he said.

Suddenly, Michaels bowled over, like someone punched him in the gut.

§

Chapter 29:1

They may hide
And they may cower,
But soon they will give in.

Michaels was slammed against the wall.

His face snapped to the right like someone slapped him.

"Ugh!" he said.

His back was shoved against the wall again.

His arm twisted behind his back.

Cursing, he hopped on one leg like someone kicked him.

"Stop it!" he yelled.

Michaels was pushed to his knees and was breathing heavily. A crowd had gathered.

He then fell face down like someone kicked his butt.

"What the hell you all looking at?" he snarled.

The crowd dispersed.

"Are you okay?" Miranda said.

"I…uh…brain seizures," he said.

"Are you hurt?"

He slapped her hand away. "I just don't like anyone telling me what to do," he said.

"Maybe we should call it a day," she suggested.

"Like I said, I don't like anyone telling me what to do."

Michaels walked with his back stiff. He seemed alright from his brain seizure. He wasn't limping.

"Come on," he said.

For someone who didn't like being told what to do, Michaels was sure bossy.

They walked on Canal Street, making their way over to the triangle where Broadway, Twenty-Third Street and Fifth Avenue meet.

"I've seen that building in old black and white movies," she said, pointing to a triangular construction that was the oddest one in Manhattan. The building was a wedge, with just one column of windows running down the backbone where two sides fanned out to make the building look like an open book. The roof of the building formed a triangle. From the sky, the building must appear like a slice of fat, lemon meringue pie.

"The Flatiron Building, an architectural wonder, given that it is still standing. The skeptics bet that, due to its shape, the wind would eventually flatten the building," he said.

The skeptics had a point about the wind. Miranda had to hold her skirt down because the wind had a tendency to rush into the triangle where the three streets met in front.

They walked leisurely the two blocks to Seventh Avenue, then up to Thirty-Fourth Street. Just east of Macy's was the Empire State Building, the tallest building in Manhattan now that the Twin Towers had fallen.

Macy's Department Store spread out across an entire block. Statues of four women stood above the R. H. MACY & CO. sign, each statue acting as architectural support.

Miranda and Michaels explored Macy's. They rode the escalators from floor to floor, up ten stories of merchandise.

"You're not like most women. The biggest department store in the world and you can't find a damned thing to buy," he said.

"I'm picky."

"And are you as picky when you choose men?"

"Only those I give my heart to," she said flirtatiously.

"And how many have you offered your heart to?"

"None," she said.

His eyes sparkled and his jaw relaxed. "Would you give me your...?" The fire went out of his eyes, and he was no longer involved in their game. His face drained of color, and his dull eyes stared like a zombie beyond Miranda. "Her," he said and groaned. But even while Michaels looked at the woman with dread, his eyes shone with love.

Miranda turned her head to see who Michaels gawked at. It could only be the woman walking with her arms full of shopping bags. She clicked her expensive high heels against the floor, her silk dress swirling and shimmering as she swayed her hips from side to side. She wore heavy red lipstick and sunglasses. A diamond necklace draped her chest. She was tall with ash blonde hair, very attractive, more handsome than pretty, but sexy. Her legs were long and muscular. She was built like an Olympic swimmer.

Miranda looked down her own slender body, delicate wrists and small-boned ankles. Her breasts were not voluptuous. He had said—you're not my type. Too skinny. Brunettes have never been my type, Lady.

Big breasted blondes. Yuck. She made a face at the woman's back.

Miranda turned back around.

There was no sign of Michaels.

§

Chapter 30:1

There will be no place to hide.

Miranda searched the rows of merchandise.

Finally, she found him. Michaels was bent over, playing with his shoelaces.

"She's coming this way," she lied with an ear-splitting grin.

He cringed, dipping his head further. A hang-dog look flattened his face.

Miranda clenched her jaw to keep from laughing because he looked so worried. "Michaels, what is it?" she whispered.

"My sister. I thought I saw my sister."

"That woman was your sister?"

He nodded his head.

She clenched her fists, thinking, *Michaels was nearly caught cheating by his wife, which is ridiculous because we have done nothing wrong.* There were his kisses in the wee hours of the morning when no one was watching, when they were confined in a carriage hidden from the world, his kisses on her hand and wrist. He had crushed his lips on hers when she fell on the street.

"You can stand up now, Michaels. Your so-called sister is gone," Miranda said, trying to sound uncaring but her words were flat.

He stood on wobbly legs.

His wife has probably had her boobs enlarged. She was phony looking, Miranda thought, smiling meanly.

Come now, Miranda. This was the voice that was so damned fair and always took both sides against her. *Michaels never said he was not married. You never had the guts to really ask him.*

Oh shut up. Don't give him the benefit of the doubt.

Still, she squeezed his arm comfortingly.

His jugular vein beat rapidly against his neck. Michaels appeared to be on the verge of a stroke.

"Michaels, are you okay?" she said in a weary voice.

Tears welled in his eyes.

"Michaels?"

He rubbed his eyes, a sigh of relief rushing from his lips. "She didn't see me," was all he said.

"No, you hid so well she wouldn't have. You must have a lot of experience hiding from women."

He blinked his damp lashes and looked at Miranda like he couldn't remember who she was.

"However, your memory is not too good. I suppose one face is the same as the next?" she said drily. Miranda let go of his arm and looked towards the exit to where the woman vanished. "Excuse me. I have to go to the ladies room."

Not that he will miss me.

Miranda staggered to the bathroom. She stared at her reflection, tracing the deep scar on her cheek that ruined her profile. *What made me think Michaels could ever be attracted to me?*

Miranda splashed cool water on her hot cheeks and reapplied her blush and lipstick. In the mirror, she watched Michaels' so-called sister exit one of the stalls.

Well, I guess her shit doesn't stink, she thought.

The woman removed her sunglasses and washed her hands. She had blue eyes and bore no resemblance to Michaels. She did, however, wear a band of gold on her left finger.

Miranda tapped her shoulder.

"Yes?" she said, raising an ash-blonde eyebrow.

"I know your brother."

"Are you a patient?"

"So, he is a therapist, or a counselor, or psychiatrist, or something?"

"No. He's an obstetrician," the woman said, smiling.

"I meant your other brother, the one who worked in the South Tower. I just had lunch with him."

"Your joke isn't funny," she said in a choked voice. She looked pale and stricken. She acted like Miranda was a worm crawling across the bathroom floor. The woman balled up her paper towel and threw it into the trash.

Okay then, Snot Nose, I know your husband. I can give you a laundry list. He's kissed me right here on my lips, on my wrist and on my palm. Miranda held up her hand to the woman's back and threw her a dirty finger as the door slammed behind the woman. It was not Miranda's finest moment.

She massaged her temples. *Mama always taught me to act like a lady,* she groaned. *Only the problem is I was just a child when she died.*

Miranda marched out of the bathroom and back to Michaels.

He didn't seem to notice that she ever left him.

§

Chapter 31:1

Heartache and decay will ride the subway.

Monday, September 24, 2001
34th Street Subway Station

Miranda stood on her tiptoes, peeking over his shoulder. "Isn't that your sister over there?"

Michaels grabbed her arm, dragging her to the furthest end of the subway platform. He stood with his back to the crowd, seeming to prefer looking at the subway walls strewn with graffiti, neglect and apathy.

She frowned at his pale face. *The coward.*

They boarded the train, and Miranda plopped down on the seat. Good thing it wasn't rush hour, else she would be flattened up against the subway window like a squashed bug. Oh yeah. That's New York City.

"Well?" he said, breaking the ice between them.

Silence. Just a look. From her this time. A cold shoulder. A toss of the head. Bingo. She hit a nerve.

"I told the truth, Mandy. I swear she is my sister."

Her again.

"Why did you hide from your sister then?" she scoffed.

He blinked his eyes.

Miranda gave him a dirty look and rubbed the scar on her cheek. Her wound was old, but the scar throbbed.

His face flushed a deep red and Michaels sat stiffly against the seat.

Miranda melted into her seat, swallowing the lump in her throat. She never felt as lonely, as she huddled in her jacket next to Michaels. Miranda never felt as small as she scanned his features; trying to detect a resemblance to the woman he claimed to be his sister. There were no similar markings between him and the woman he hid from at the mall, the woman who affected him so deeply, even now the cords of his neck were taut. He clenched his jaw, pretending to sleep. The sorrow weighing down his shoulders was palpable.

What a fiasco the other day when he kissed me.

Don't. Don't touch me, he had said.

Michaels was thinking about his wife. Maybe the golden woman is the reason he drinks.

His reaction to the woman at the mall unraveled her. From the first, Miranda thought of the woman as a rival.

She gulped. *A rival? For what?*

You mean for whom. Quit acting coy and be honest with yourself.

She wasn't such a fool to believe every word sung to her by a man she barely knew. Nor was Miranda such an idiot to think she could be Michael's soul mate, married or not. But just sitting near him twisted her insides until the train stopped at the Rockefeller Center Station.

They walked along the subway plank, Michaels deep in thought.

"Yipes!" he yelled, flinging his legs up. Michaels fell across the subway tracks like someone threw him.

"Michaels!" she screamed.

A train roared up the tracks, towards him.

Michaels just lay there, staring at the train like he had a death wish.

§

Chapter 32:1

And from the ashes will arise a new city.

"Michaels! Michaels!" she cried.

He lay there on the tracks, looking at her and then at the train headed towards him.

"Michaels! Oh God, "Michaels!"

The heat from the approaching train was scorching and Miranda closed her eyes, screaming his name repeatedly.

She could feel the heat from the passing train.

"Michaels!" she cried. *Oh, my God, he's dead!*

Someone tapped her shoulder.

"I'm okay," he said. Michaels stood on the platform beside her.

"But how did you…?" She hiccupped, her throat choked with tears.

"I have lightning reflexes, and you are crying so hard that your tears block your vision."

Miranda clung to him, rubbing his arms and chest. *I almost lost him.*

"I'm fine," he said and grabbed her wrists, flinging them at her sides.

He stormed away with his head hanging down.

Miranda followed somberly behind Michaels, up Sixth Avenue.

He stopped at the Jekyll & Hyde Club on Avenue of the Americas.

"Stay," he ordered Ashes.

The little dog rolled over like he was playing dead.

The exterior of The Jekyll & Hyde Club resembled an old mansion lifted as a backdrop from an Indiana Jones movie and plopped down in the middle of Manhattan.

"This restaurant is supposed to be haunted. There are creatures from the spirit world," he whispered.

He opened the massive club door and pushed her in.

"Boo!" he said.

He slapped his knee, chuckling at her expression.

"Sorry," she muttered, "but I'm still a bit touchy about ghosts. I've been having dreams."

He held up his hands like Frankenstein. "Ooh, supernatural visitations!" His eyes were laughing at her.

She playfully punched his arm.

There was a lit case of skulls.

Pictures with eyes followed them.

Portraits of Frankenstein and his doctor hung on the wall.

"This is where Lyle decided to become a gynecologist. I think the club convinced my brother what fun it would be to become an archaeologist, but the blondes convinced him being a gynecologist would be even more fun," he said.

Oh no. Here we go with the blondes again, she thought, frowning at the blonde hostess.

"We had such great times here, me and Lyle. It's safe to sit down. Lyle should still be at work," he said.

"We can eat here because your brother is at work?"

"Lyle always makes a play for my girl," he said, giving her a wicked grin.

Her jaw dropped at being labeled his girl. *Of course, he's joking.*

Michaels wiggled his butt more comfortably in his seat. "My parents were proud of Lyle. The only time we could get along was at a bar, the drunken rambling of two brothers fighting for their birthright. Other times, we barely acknowledged the other was alive. 'How about Jekyll and Hyde's', Lyle would say. We'd drink our supper and then take turns carrying the other home."

Whatever memories bothered him in the subway, Michaels seemed to have exorcised. He had a devil-may-care, screw-the-world attitude. "I'll have a yard of beer," he told the waitress.

"Maybe you shouldn't drink so much," Miranda said.

"Maybe you should mind your own business," he snapped.

"A glass of your house wine, Pinot Noir," Miranda told the waitress. She added appetizers to their order to counter the effects of alcohol on empty stomachs. She handed the waitress the menus. "Is it normally this crowded for so early in the day?"

The waitress said, "Since 9/11 a lot of people are drinking away their fears, pain, stress, and the uncertainty. There is no way us New Yorkers are going to run away and abandon our city. We will all go down with our ship, drunk if we must stay, but New Yorkers loyal to the very end."

"Here. Here," Michaels said. "Add a shot of whiskey to my order."

Miranda gave him a look.

"Make that a double," he said, holding up two fingers and grinning at Miranda.

The waitress winked at him and he slapped her butt. She sashayed away to place their order.

"What did you and your brother fight over? A woman?" Miranda said.

He snorted. "Women are so self-centered they believe the world revolves around them."

The waitress returned, setting on the floor beside him a yard of beer.

He twisted the three-foot tall glass, so the beer would flow slowly, and took a gulp. "Ah. Now that's good," he said, lifting the beer and taking a very long drink.

She eyed his Adam's apple bobbing as he swallowed.

"Don't worry. I haven't fallen off the wagon," he said wryly, wiping the back of his mouth with his hand.

"Why are you drinking so much then? Are the memories too much for you?"

He scoffed.

"Guilt?"

His complexion grayed. "Why do you say that?" he whispered.

"Your wife must be unhappy about you spending so much time with me," she said coldly.

He rolled his eyes like she was fishing.

The awkward moment was saved by a large slab lowered from the ceiling of the restaurant. On the slab lay the figure of Frankenstein.

Dr. Madd stepped up to the monster in an attempt to bring it to life. The doctor was one of the many characters roaming the Jekyll & Hyde club, entertaining guests or harassing them, depending on one's point of view.

"Is there life after death?" Miranda mused.

"If you're looking for answers, ask Fang the Gargoyle," Michaels said, pointing to an ugly, stone, devilish creature sitting cross-legged on the wall, clasping an eerie looking ball with long, claw-like fingers. "They claim Fang guards the portal between this world and the nether world."

"Well, Fang, is there life after death?" she said.

Smoke vaporized around the gargoyle, one of many eerie mechanical marvels at the Jekyll & Hyde Club. His eyes glowed red and his jaws moved as he spoke of Dr. Victor Frankenstein's castle, Fang's original home centuries ago. Fang told the tale of how he ended up in the middle of Manhattan in this century.

"Not a decent castle to be had in all of Manhattan. Rent control. My master will be down shortly," Fang said with a nasally, vibrating voice meant to scare but laughable. His eyes darkened, smoke evaporating into the bowels of the restaurant.

Michaels lifted the yard glass to his mouth, swirling the beer. "Now watch, the tricky part is when the glass begins to empty. I tilt the glass back even further, while trying not to drown my face with beer," he said, grinning in triumph because he neatly swallowed a mouthful. "Here. You try."

She lifted the yard glass to her lips, swirling it like Michaels had. Laughing, she turned the glass too fast and beer ran down the long skinny neck, spilling across her mouth and drenching her.

He dabbed at her mouth with a napkin.

They stared at one another, neither daring to breathe.

Until a man stepped up to their table. "Ah. Young lovers," he said in a Dracula accent. "Allow me to introduce myself. I am Count Vladimir von Trope of Transylvania."

"Don't you mean Pennsylvania?" Michaels said dryly.

The Count dashed at her neck with his fangs, and she screeched. The Count then moved onto the next table.

"Where did Jake go to college?" she said. If Michaels got skittish at the mention of her brother, she would walk out of this place and leave him washing dishes to pay the check.

"I don't remember. Probably NYU but Jacob wasn't in my class. I'm older and didn't know him then."

"Perhaps he wasn't living here then," she said, eyeing his NYU graduation ring on his right hand.

"You should check the records of the college in Austin."

"I have checked with the University of Texas."

They munched on a couple of hamburgers. He chewed his food slowly, glancing suspiciously at her from time to time.

She would smile at him and he would grin back, but his smile appeared phony.

He's bored with me and patronizing. Michaels is merely tolerating my presence.

Miranda waited impatiently for the waitress to return her credit card.

She didn't realize how smashed Michaels was until he staggered out of Jekyll & Hyde's. He fell to his knees and crawled on the sidewalk.

Miranda knelt, helping him to rise.

"Sorry," he slurred and kept apologizing.

"Stay there while I get a cab."

He saluted her and laughed, holding his stomach.

She moved over in the cab to make room for him.

"Watch your head," she said, but he banged his noggin against the cab anyway.

Michaels fell across the seat, dropping his head on her lap.

He was snoring, passed out. She resisted the urge to play with his hair.

The driver pulled over to the Algonquin. Michaels abruptly sat up. He jerked open the door and jumped out. Michaels stumbled on the curb. He held onto the trunk, unsteady on his feet.

"Just get in the cab, Michaels, and I'll pay the driver to take you home," she said.

He yanked out that beaten wallet from his pants. Michaels pulled out a credit card.

"Here," he said, wobbling.

The driver took the credit card.

Michaels signed the receipt and stuffed a copy in his pocket.

He walked crookedly into her hotel. At least he wasn't crawling.

Miranda picked up his credit card receipt that had fallen out of his pocket and stuffed it in her purse.

§

Chapter 33:1

And the weak will help the strong,
And the strong the weak.
They will lean upon each other
So neither shall fall.

Monday, September 24, 2001
The Oak Room at the Algonquin Hotel

Miranda and Michaels sat at a high table. Their knees pressed together, feeling like a pulse beat at her kneecap, pumping blood up her thigh to the darkness of the bar. The solitude, the proximity and the confined corner were too much for her senses.

And then there was him.

Michaels dug his elbows into the wood and ordered a glass of soda water for himself and wine for Miranda.

The waitress set two glasses of Merlot on the table.

"Trying to get me drunk, Michaels?" she said in a reckless voice.

"Do I look like the type of man who has to get a woman drunk?"

"Yes."

"Liar," he said, grinning.

"I'd like to drown you in this glass of wine," she said sweetly.

He sat there cool and cocky, looking more sober with each passing minute. There was a defiant look in his eyes.

She rubbed her scar and suddenly had a headache. "I am tired. Unless you tell me about Jake, I am going up to my room."

"One dance before we say good night then," he said, pushing his chair back. He held a hand out.

Miranda chewed her bottom lip. Michaels was so damned attractive, and she was lonely.

He could have been hit by that train at the subway station. Michaels might have died.

Quit playing with fire.

It's necessary to spend time in his company to find out about Jake. My time is running out.

You want him for yourself, not because of Jake. You have spent time with Michaels for the last few days and didn't press him that much about Jake.

But his black outs…his memory lapse.

You've been acting like he's your date. You want to believe Michaels spends time with you, not because you are Jake's sister but because he is attracted to you.

For Jake, she insisted. Miranda should be thinking of letting go of Jake, not of losing Michaels.

But I'm leaving soon. Surely one dance won't hurt.

She placed her hand in his, feeling light-headed.

He led her to the dance floor.

The Oak Room was a jazz place and the band was playing Louis Armstrong's *What a Wonderful World.*

Miranda rested her cheek on his shoulder.

They moved slowly, almost floating in a corner.

In a surreal moment, everyone else on the crowded dance floor faded. Even the music sounded as if it played far away, growing fainter, yet their feet moved, and Michaels swung her around the room.

She buried her face in his shoulder. His silky hair smelled like the peaches Michaels claimed he had been eating before the planes hit the Twin Towers.

He rubbed his forehead against her ear, inhaling her perfume. The balls of his thumbs circled the hollows of her collar bone.

Her hand delved beneath the collar of his shirt, playing with the hair on his neck. "You need a haircut," she whispered.

"So do you. But don't ever cut your hair. I like it just the way it is."

"Messy?"

"Wild," he said, biting her ear, just a nibble. Enough to make her want to give him more, until she was consumed by him, and he had his fill of her.

Oh, God, I've had too much to drink!

The song ended but they danced all by themselves in the middle of the floor.

When the music began, they stopped dancing and just talked. They stood in the middle of the dance floor never taking their eyes from each other, hearing no other voices, and seeing no one else.

The music again ended, yet they danced, the only couple on the floor. Music enveloped them, notes only heard by them. The room spun in slow motion, as if time stood still, as if they stood still and the world danced around them.

"You fill my head with magic," he said.

"You're drunk."

"I am intoxicated by the sight of you, windblown, wild and sweet," he said, lifting her hand to his lips. Michaels sucked on her pinky, rubbing his thumb across her hand. He drew her to his chest until they breathed the same air.

Miranda swayed against him. She would fall if he let her go.

He massaged her ear with his lips. "You're the most beautiful woman I've ever seen."

"I think you're wonderful," she said, blushing at his lop-sided grin.

Miranda ignored her first impression and intuition that seduction was Michaels' game, and he was the expert. She conveniently overlooked her suspicion that he probably had a wife. She brushed off the number of drinks he guzzled and his yard of beer—the fact that he crawled from Jekyll and Hyde's. All she could concentrate on were his hands pressing against her rear end, making her forgetful of others in the room, and what they must think of his fingers sliding up her blouse. Respect was the last thing Miranda craved, now, here, with this man.

He can respect me in the morning, if morning ever comes.

Michaels squeezed her collar bones, massaging her shoulders. His hands burned through her brassiere straps where his fingers branded her skin.

Her bones turned to jelly. She moaned.

His lips stroked her ear. "Which room is yours?"

§

Chapter 34:1

And it will seem as if there will be no tomorrow.

His breath swirled around her hair and Miranda could hardly breathe, much less remember her room number. "The twelfth floor," she finally stammered.

They held hands, clinging to each other's fingers as they floated towards the elevators.

When the elevator doors snapped shut, Michaels imprisoned her hand behind her back, yanking her against him.

He ran his tongue across her jaw line. "For days I've wanted to devour you and wondered what flavor you would be if I gave into my desire to gobble you up," he said, nibbling her lips. "You taste of honey, soft, sweet and pure like water flowing down the mountain on the first day of spring. I have no will, when I am with you. Are you trying to tame me, Mandy?"

"No woman could ever tame you, Michaels," she said, breathlessly.

"Until now. No woman could make me want only her, burn for just her. Your eyes drown me, and I've had a hard time coming up for air since I first saw you, touched you, and thought of no one else. The odor of your perfumed soap drifted up to my nose that first day—your scent was clean, fresh and innocent. You feel like velvet, purple royal velvet, the kind that when wrapped around a man's body spoils him so that nothing else will ever do for him again. I'm turning into a romantic, something I swore I would never do. Romance is for fools. Reality has always been my game," he said, closing his eyes and groaning.

"Have I really tamed you," she said in a voice that would break, if he played with her.

His answer was to act like an animal. He smashed his lips against her lips.

She wildly kissed him back, grabbing onto his belt and pushing her hips into his.

He squeezed her tighter, lifting her off the ground, riding her skirt up and massaging her thigh.

Her feet dangled in mid-air but Miranda was mostly aware of his lips.

His tongue.

His teeth.

The muscles across his back.

His chest pushing against her breasts.

The buckle of his belt.

The zipper of his pants.

His hard thigh pushing between her legs.

His hand riding higher up the back of her skirt. Groping. Tugging.

The kiss went on and on.

She wrapped her legs around his waist, shoving into him.

Michaels kept kissing her and humping his hips against hers while he reached behind, feeling for the elevator button.

She kissed his neck, moaning.

He cupped her buttocks, running his thumbs along the elastic of her underpants. He kissed her rakishly, drawing her into him and grinding into her.

Miranda's heart slammed against her ribs, her breath escaping in gasps. She gripped his arms, feeling his muscles bulge beneath his shirt. Michaels was strong, and he could probably break her in two if he wanted, physically.

Just don't break me. Emotionally. Spiritually.

The elevator bell rang and the doors popped open.

He took a deep breath and tensed his muscles.

Miranda spread her fingers across his back, lowering her eyes to his body. Michaels was dressed in a white silk shirt with no t-shirt. He was damp with sweat so his shirt plastered him like a second skin. Muscles rippled across his broad chest, narrowing to a small waist. She could make out the hairs curling from his neck all the way down to his navel. The hair crept down his stomach and disappeared inside the bulge of his pants.

Even with his obvious state of arousal, Michaels managed to punch the elevator, backwards, so they would land on the twelfth floor.

Miranda lowered her feet to the elevator floors and back to earth. "How much practice does it take a wolf to learn that trick?" she said in a shaky voice.

He pressed his forehead against hers. "I'm not the big bad wolf. I'm not a wolf any longer, not anymore, not since I met you."

Not a wolf since he met me? Since just five days before?

All this time Michaels acted like a wolf hunting her, albeit a well-groomed wolf with blonde hair smelling of peaches. Occasionally, he was a polite, well mannered wolf.

Michaels gave her a wolfish grin, and her insides turned to jelly at the desire in his eyes. Not since I met you, he had said. Miranda wanted to act foolish and tell him, I think I love you, but she had been stupid with men before. This feeling was different—every other man in her life paled and faded into the walls of this hotel. Miranda couldn't risk playing the fool with this man, never with Michaels.

Then why did you invite him up to your room?

Only to talk.

Yeah. Right. What about his wife, you lame-brain idiot.

Shut up. I don't know for sure that he's married.

Ask him.

Shut up.

Miranda demurely handed him her key and would have plunged through the elevator doors if he hadn't taken her hand.

Michaels pulled her across the hallway.

Miranda couldn't feel the floor so she kicked her shoes off, leaving her pumps wherever. She still floated, her insides quivering, and her heart beating so slowly, surely she must be dreaming.

With steady hands he unlocked the door, flicking on the light switch.

She dizzily looked around a hotel room decorated with antiques. Miranda was so lightheaded that she would not have known it was her room except for Ashes, whom she brought up earlier. The dog scurried so fast to the bathroom; he seemed to vanish into thin air.

One wall of the room was a bay window brilliantly lit by the background of Manhattan's skyline. Jake's ghost was not hanging outside the window to make her feel guilty about forgetting about her brother.

Don't think about Jake. Tomorrow, I promise.

Michaels turned to her and his face lit up more radiant than the room. Desire shone from his eyes, a flame igniting her own fire.

She was the first to look away, her eyes settling on the bed. Miranda counted the stripes on the green and black bedspread. *One. Two. Three. Four…*

Michaels moved closer so his breath stroked her hair. "Mandy," he whispered like there was joy in her name. "My Mandy."

Just her name from his lips made her moan as he drew her into his arms where night became day, where she brightened like the sun. Michaels hugged her like he might never let her go. He smiled gently. "I've been waiting for you for so long, a lifetime," he said, cupping her face with his hands. He looked deep into her eyes.

She mewed back.

"I confess I've wanted this from the very first. I planned your seduction, like you were a thousand-piece puzzle I needed to solve. I've wanted you so desperately; I tore down your defenses one by one," he said, grinning wolfishly.

He cradled her head, crushing her lips with his.

Moaning, she wrapped her arms around his neck, bringing him closer until Michaels leaned into her. He dipped to her collar bone, suckling the hollow of her shoulder. Miranda covered her breast with his hand and squeezed his fingers.

She unbuttoned the top four buttons of her blouse.

He shoved his hand into her bra, massaging her, twirling and squeezing. He yanked her strap down her shoulder so her breast hung half-way from its harness with nothing between his mouth and her but a thin cotton blouse. Michaels lowered his head, nibbling at her blouse, sucking her nipple right through the cloth.

The sensation was more erotic than if his mouth was directly on her bare skin. Michaels couldn't even wait to undress her.

Be sensible. He acts like he moved heaven and earth to be with you. More like his wife out of the way.

Her ability to reason weakened as her legs turned to jelly. Sanity was fleeting as Miranda swayed in his arms. That this should be happening to her was amazing, that Michaels should feel more than desire for her. She could read his want in his eyes, hear his need in his heart beats that whispered to Miranda not to deny her intuition, not to fight the fact that Michaels was pulling her forward into himself. He was sucking her into his very being, inside his own essence, until their souls touched and she was beneath his skin, their hearts beating as one.

"I need this. I need you. And the rest be damned," he growled.

Michaels cupped her face with his hands and kissed her forehead, her nose, and her cheeks. Miranda thought she heard him whisper, "I'm sorry, Mandy," before his mouth swallowed hers.

"What?" she mumbled.

She clung to his neck, belt, and shirt.

His lips traveled over her body.

She went limp, vaguely thinking, *what were his last words?*

Miranda thought she heard a knocking at the window. *Jake? What is it? What are you trying to tell me?*

Michaels buried his face in her shoulder, swinging her into his arms.

What was it Michaels said? What? What?

He kissed the palm of her hand, and Miranda forgot about everything else.

Michaels carried her over to the bed and slowly lowered her, sliding her body down his. His hands fumbled with the buttons of her blouse.

"You're going to tear them," she said, unhooking the last button, her fingers as anxious as his.

Michaels fanned open her blouse, exposing her chest. He cupped a breast in each hand, burying his face in her neck, rubbing both breasts against his cheeks. He ran his hands down the sides of her body, playing her ribs like piano keys. His hot breath fanned her neck.

He leaned his body into hers, making her hot. The smell of peaches from his silky hair made her dizzy.

But most of all there was—him.

His tongue outlined her cheek bone. He pried open her mouth with his lips.

She wildly kissed him back.

His hand dived beneath her skirt. He slid his palm across her nylons, pushing her skirt up until he found her garter belt. He walked his fingers to her bare skin, his hand burning her cool thigh.

He impatiently parted her knees with his leg.

His kisses intensified, the tip of his tongue outlining the inside of her mouth.

Michaels was ambidextrous and knew his way around a woman's body as if he drew the map. He ripped off her blouse, and then stood behind her, kissing her back, sliding his moist lips down her spine. His tongue traveled upward from the base of her spine.

She moaned, melting beneath his moist mouth.

Michaels plopped on the bed and stood her between his legs. His tongue slid across her back while his hands slid up her thighs, exploring her like a centipede with power to delve beneath skin and play a woman like an instrument. He stroked the right keys. Miranda flung back her head and cried out his name, aching with need.

His arms tightened against her stomach and she metamorphosed in his arms. Michaels was her sculptor and Miranda his clay as she allowed him to remold her in any fashion he chose.

He became impatient, pulled her to her feet, and yanked her skirt off, peeling her black slip down her hips.

Miranda locked her eyes with his and pushed his hair from his forehead, her eyes sparkling at the vulnerable look in his eyes. Michaels let down his guard for her.

Their hearts sounded like two drummers beating in time.

The walls of this hotel room were not thick enough to hold back the fire inflaming them both with a passion so strong it overwhelmed, hurling them into another dimension where only they existed. Nothing else. No past. Just this moment. Now. A lifetime.

Never taking her eyes from his, Miranda removed her last item of clothing, exposing herself to his eyes. She was naked and never felt so vulnerable.

Michaels stroked her hips, pulling her toward him. He massaged her thighs, staring up at her face, his eyes glazed over with passion. He groaned, running his tongue around her belly button. Michaels dipped his head further and she gasped. He buried his face in her and Miranda arched like a bow, swinging her hair across her back as she pushed herself into him, holding the top of his head so she wouldn't fall as her legs weakened.

He held her tighter and shoved his head against her, moaning into her. "You taste of honey, just as I imagined, exactly like I tasted in my dreams," he said.

Her legs buckled and Michaels braced her. He rolled his thumbs into her hip bones. His mouth writhed against Miranda, not allowing her to free herself before he should drive her crazy with his tongue.

She screamed on and on. "Ah. Ah. Ah." Miranda tried to shout out his name, but no coherent word could pass her lips as she lost all control and the room spun.

His laughter muffled against her, glorying in his power that he could bring her to her knees, to the point where she would do anything for him. Miranda was his slave, hanging limp in his arms, the aftermath of his lovemaking.

Though still numb, Miranda slowly recovered and kicked her underwear from around her foot. She sat in his lap, wrapping her ankles around his waist. She drifted in and out of haziness, a world where bones turn to liquid. She floated without a head, all tingling nerves and senses.

His smell of peaches drifted up to her nose. She ran her hands down the ripples of his back, shivering from the feel of his muscles.

Michaels kissed her as he unbuttoned his shirt.

She pulled impatiently at his belt buckle.

"Sh. Not so fast. We've plenty of time," he said.

"Uh, do you have protection?"

He emptied his pockets, scattering the contents on the nightstand—not much there.

"Don't worry," he said, "I've been fixed."

Miranda whispered into his ear and he groaned, fell back on the bed, and squeezed his eyes tightly, his breath coming in gasps and groans. Michaels sounded like he was in pain.

Miranda ran a fingernail down his chest, scratching at his skin and teasing him.

His eyes dilated. He breathed rapidly as though it hurt to move his chest.

She lay down beside him, lifting her leg over his. Miranda ran her hand down his chest, tugging at the hair that grew there, and tracing with her fingernail a line running across his side from his chest to beneath his ribs. She balanced on her knees and licked his scar. "What happened?" she said.

"I'd rather not talk about it," he said, frowning.

"What about this?" she said, flicking her tongue across another scar rippling across his chest.

"Lyle."

"Brotherly love, huh? And this?" she said, examining his left wrist and burn that looked fresh like the skin was recently charred.

Michaels gave her the oddest look. He rubbed his wrist like it still pained him. "I was drunk. My fingers weren't too steady when I lit a cigarette," he mumbled.

"I didn't know you smoked."

"I don't remember," he said with a peculiar look in his dazed eyes.

"Please don't have a blackout now," she begged, sliding her hand to his stomach.

"I'm just having a hard time concentrating," he panted.

Michaels flung her across the bed. "Mandy," he groaned. His breathing was even more ragged. He gripped her wrists, lifting them above her head. Their tongues met and melded.

She locked her lips on his, rolled over and sat on his chest, straddling him and wiggling against him.

He moaned like a wounded animal.

Miranda laughed seductively, rubbing her nose against his and rocking on him. "I have you right where I've always wanted you," she said.

"Always?" he grunted, his eyes gleaming. His voice sounded winded.

"Well not always. I must confess I didn't like you at first."

Michaels threw her on her back, kneeling above her. "And now? What do you think of me now?"

"I can't stand you," she groaned.

His eyes roamed the length of her body still flushed and damp from his lovemaking. "I wondered what you'd look like. You're more beautiful than I imagined."

"When did you wonder?"

"When I first saw you at Ground Zero."

"When I ran into you?"

"No. Before. I was watching you the whole time."

"You are beautiful," she said, breathlessly, outlining his full lips with her fingernail.

His responding laughter was husky. "You think I'm beautiful?"

Miranda nodded. "You are the most beautiful man I have ever seen," she said, running a hand down his chiseled cheek. Her other hand caressed his chest.

Miranda wrapped her legs around his waist. She poked his ear with her tongue. "Come into my parlor, said the spider to the fly."

Michaels growled and rammed into her.

"I love you. I love you," she moaned.

He stopped moving.

Silence was never so loud. Miranda regretted speaking impetuously. Perhaps, she made a grave mistake, offering this man her heart.

"Don't look at me with so much trust," he moaned. Anguish replaced the lust in his eyes and a tortured groan escaped his lips. "Mandy," was all he said, like a prayer.

It was enough. It had to be enough as Miranda drew him into her, deeper, until Michaels was so far inside, all he could do was make love to her like a man possessed.

Afterwards, he lay with an arm thrown across his face.

She nestled between his other arm and his chest with her leg lifted over his.

Michaels entwined her fingers with his and squeezed. "And the rest be damned, like I am," he mumbled.

"What?" Miranda said, even though she heard.

"Go to sleep, Mandy," he said, wearily. "Just go to sleep."

Their breathing slowed, returning to a more natural rhythm, but his heart still beat rapidly against her ear.

"Mandy?"

"Mm?"

Michaels squeezed her hand, and she thought her bones would break before he relaxed. He folded her in his arms and they lay like two spoons. "Let's get some sleep. It's late," he murmured against her hair.

Breath rushed from between her lips like a balloon deflated. She closed her eyes, rubbing her cheek against his arm.

He switched off the lamp.

Michaels closed his eyes until he sensed Miranda had fallen asleep. He threw the covers off and rose from the bed. He tucked her in like she was a child, and then yanked up his pants and walked over to the window. He stared out at the lights of the city.

He had been a cynical, distrustful, fast-paced, cool, hot-shot, New York stock broker chasing the gold. 9/11 had changed him in more ways than one. Before the attacks, Michaels never would have fallen in love. Well he might have. After all, he was as human as the next man. But he never would have admitted it to himself or anyone else. Michaels would have fought against love and probably would have won, not realizing he lost in the process. Oh, he was okay with marrying for money, but love?

But now everything was different. He was different. Michaels appreciated family and friends. He hadn't even realized before how much he loved this city. His city. The smells. The sounds. The heart of the city beating at Times Square. The laughter and tears of Broadway. The expectations of off-Broadway. The hopes and dreams of New Yorkers and even the newly arrived.

Like so many others, Michaels had merely used Manhattan, taking it for granted and never giving back anything but taxes. Hereafter, there would forever be a *Before 9/11* and an *After 9/11*. It all meant so much to him now.

Michaels looked away from the lights of the city and over to where she slept. He cared for this woman in ways he could never have imagined. They hadn't just made love. This wasn't merely a man and a woman reaching out blindly in the dark with lust. Within the confines of this hotel room their minds melded, and their souls merged.

Michaels clenched the frame of the window so tightly, veins protruded from his fingers. His face stared back at him from the window pane reflecting an agony worse than death. *I've broken my own heart,* he mouthed. *I should have stayed away from her.* Michaels flattened his head against the window. *It wasn't supposed to turn out this way.*

He ran his fingers through his hair and paced silently in the room. He was a coward and a fool.

Michaels walked over to the bed and stood over Miranda. He clenched and unclenched his fists. He reached out a hand to her then withdrew.

Miranda stirred restlessly in her sleep.

He quietly opened the minibar, taking out every alcoholic beverage in the fridge. Michaels guzzled each small bottle, swallowing the burning liquid.

He straddled a chair, waiting for the sun to rise, holding his head and wishing there was more to drink. There wasn't enough alcohol in the world to numb his pain.

Michaels flung his arms across the back of the chair. A haggard look tortured his pale face. His heart twisted as he watched her sleep.

A peaceful smile lightened her face, making Miranda look like a little girl.

His head drooped to his chest, and a heartfelt sigh escaped his lips.

His fortune had read: he who manipulates fate gets what he deserves.

Oh, Mandy, what have I done?

Michaels held his face in his hands, groaning.

§

Chapter 35:1

And hearts will bleed.

Tuesday, September 26, 2001

Miranda didn't want to wake from a pleasant dream where she and Michaels were having a picnic in a golden field of yellow flowers. His head rested on her lap, and she stroked his cheek. He smiled up at her. The valley was so peaceful they would spend eternity here, just the two of them, alone in the world. She only needed him, just him.

Miranda stirred in her sleep, slowly becoming aware of her surroundings. She extended her arms above her head, stretching and smiling. She reached out a hand to the pillow beside her. Except for her, the bed was empty.

She jerked to a sitting position as panic tightened her chest.

The bathroom door was open, but silence came from that direction.

A painting of yellow flowers hung on the wall. Standing in the field of flowers was a woman holding a blue hat. Her hair was blown about by the wind. A sad smile twisted the woman's lips. The woman looked all alone, as if her lover deserted her.

The bedspread was thrown on the floor.

The rug was still maroon with a Victorian print.

The lamp and telephone were on the end table, but there was no message light flickering, like a heart swinging from hope to despair.

The pad of note paper was blank. There was an envelope, a hotel pen but no written message.

The rose she had placed in a vase was dead, its petals dried, the stem turning brown.

I must be blind to not have seen him, she thought, breathing a sigh of relief. Her skin colored to a silly red. It seemed Michaels had been there all along, relaxed in a chair with his arms folded across his chest and a grim look in his eyes. *On second thought, his body is taut with tension. He does not appear happy to see me.*

But Michaels is here, in my room. He hasn't abandoned me.

Miranda yawned and hugged her knees to her chest. She wiggled her toes, giggling like a school girl. It must be mid-morning. She rubbed her eyes at sunlight shining through the bay window, but no amount of rubbing could wash away the brightness shining from inside her because of Michaels, even given that he was fully clothed. His shirt and pants were rumpled as if he slept in his clothes. His chin was slumped in his hands. Michaels appeared as if he had not gotten any sleep. He looked haggard and disturbed, like maybe he should be committed which is exactly what she would like from him, to get some kind of commitment about what he felt for her. The idea wasn't that crazy. After all, Miranda hadn't invented the word. Eve coined the word commitment—something to do about a man named Adam and an apple.

Miranda stretched lazily, arching her back. "Good morning," she said cheerfully. She would not let his sour mood stop her from singing. "Woke up on the wrong side of the bed, have we?" she said, echoing his words of a few days before.

He grunted.

"Or perhaps you fell off the bed?" she said, pointing her chin at the bedspread flung across the floor.

Silence. He gave her a black look.

"Don't tell me you're one of those men who makes love to a woman and then leaves before breakfast," she said, lifting an eyebrow.

Michaels sat down beside her, the mattress creaking from his weight. He folded her hands in his and smiled a half effort. "I'd like to have you for breakfast, sleepy head."

She rose to her knees and hugged him.

He rested his cheek atop her head.

Miranda ran the back of her hand down his grizzled cheek.

Michaels flinched as if she hurled him into a cold shower.

Her eyes softened while his eyes became bleaker, a stormy ocean of gray. A tortured groan rose from his chest. He broke out into a cold sweat.

Michaels jumped from the mattress, pacing across the rug.

Finally, he stopped walking. Michaels visibly trembled with his mouth wide open as if he wanted to speak, but all that came from between his lips was a squawk. He appeared to be choking.

She moved to go to him.

He held out a hand to stop her.

She crossed her arms in front of her chest, tapping her red painted toenail against the rug. "Are you going to plead another blackout?" she said, frowning at the empty bottles scattered across the floor. Exactly how much of a minibar tab had Michaels run up?

"I remember everything between us," he said. "Every word said, each day. You think I'll ever forget anything about last night?"

"I don't know. You tell me."

"Sit, Miranda."

The tone of his voice was so cold she obeyed. Miranda yanked the covers to her chin. Her teeth chattered, and Goosebumps erupted on her arms. The name Miranda sounded like a curse from his lips. What happened to Mandy, spoken last night like an endearment? Michaels had always used her nickname like an intimate friend. Never before did he call her by her formal name.

Michaels placed both hands beside the headboard, trapping her on the bed. He lifted her chin with his finger, smiling harshly down at her. His gray eyes that burned with fire for her last night, which looked so cold minutes ago, appeared in the throes of agony. The veins of his eyes were bloodshot. His voice was hoarse and dry. "I'm a hard man, Miranda. I didn't expect to feel this way about any woman. I never felt this way before. Believe me when I say, I need you more than you need me. That this should happen to me now is one of the great ironies. I just wanted you to know how I feel before I tell you that I can never see you again."

He let go of her chin and stared down at Miranda with his fists balled into his pockets and his flesh safely out of harm's way.

§

Chapter 36:1

There is a big hole in America's heart,
An even bigger hole in mine.

Oh, God, I'm acting like a baby. Hold back your tears! Don't cry in front of him!

Miranda reached over to the nightstand for a tissue.

What the…?

She was holding the receipt for the taxi cab last night—Michael's credit card receipt that he tried to stuff into his pocket and instead dropped on the curb.

She read the name on the Master Card receipt: Jacob Balboa.

Jake? Michaels has Jake's credit card?

"You thief!" she screamed at him.

Miranda threw the notepad, pen and envelope that were on the end table at him.

Michaels ducked.

"You bastard! What did you do to my brother?" she yelled, throwing the receipt at him.

"Oh, shit! I really was hammered last night!" he said, noting her brother's name.

She jumped from the bed, pummeling his chest with her fists.

He simply took her abuse.

Her eyes were wild, his own eyes filled with anguish.

Michaels grabbed her wrists to subdue her.

Miranda kicked at his shin, struggling to free herself while he hopped on one leg.

Finally, she exhausted herself.

They were both breathing heavily.

"I'm going to call the police," she said.

Michaels looked at the credit card receipt and cringed. "I can explain."

"Oh, yeah? Did you rob Jake?"

He raised his eyes to the ceiling. "Fuck!"

"Did you kill my brother?" she hollered.

He flinched, his face pale. "I said there is an explanation. I never meant for this to happen, for you to be here alone with me where there were no crowds to stop us. I suspected you were in love with me before you ever mouthed the words. I knew you were falling in love with me before we came up to this room, but I slept with you anyway, which makes my sin greater."

What sin does he mean? He murdered Jake! I slept with my brother's killer! She cringed, shrinking inside.

Michaels looked guilty, like a man in line for the electric chair. "I never should have touched you. Last night, I should have left your hotel and walked away from you. Twenty steps. That's all it would have taken. Twenty steps and you would never have seen me again. I couldn't help myself, Miranda. Last night, you writhed in my arms like I was the drug you craved. I've always been a selfish bastard. I take what I want."

"Like Jake's credit card!"

His eyes were tortured. "I wanted you more than I ever wanted anything. Believe me when I say, I never deliberately meant to deceive you."

"What exactly did you mean not to happen? You insisted on coming to my hotel last night. Remember your words that you planned this almost from the very start. Now you say you never meant for it to happen?"

"I did want it to happen. Subconsciously, I did plan this but never meant to carry my seduction through. You don't know how many times I wrestled with my conscience."

"Oh, so you have a conscience. What about Jake? What about my brother?" she cried out.

"Maybe it was the booze. I never should have touched the liquor. Whiskey always makes me crazy, especially now."

Miranda folded in half, hugging her stomach and moaning. *Michaels made love to me because he was drunk? Was he drunk when he killed Jake? His blackouts are the result of alcohol bingeing!*

"Please don't look at me like that. I don't regret one moment of our time together. I refuse to cheapen the act between us with repentance," he said.

Miranda reached out a hand to the end table to support herself. Michaels called their love making an act. Well, he was right. It had all been an act on his part.

Michaels focused his eyes on her nakedness, looking as muddled as she felt.

"Oh," she exclaimed, grabbing a robe. Miranda pulled the belt of a white fluffy, terry-cloth robe tightly around her waist, fanning the collar around her neck.

He pulled at his hair. "Can't you understand? Have you any idea? Didn't you listen to anything I've said? When a man is responsible because of a tragic situation, he has to live with that guilt for all eternity," he said, his voice trembling.

"I don't follow you. What are you talking about, Michaels? You hinted that you knew how my brother died. Did you kill Jake or not?"

Michaels looked physically ill. "No," he said, but looked really, really guilty.

Michaels didn't come entirely clean. He is still hiding something from me. What did he do to Jake?

He sighed, running a hand through his hair. "Sit down, Miranda. I don't want you fainting on me."

Michaels rummaged through his pants pocket, yanking out a wallet in bad shape. The wallet was the same one she'd seen in his hands when Miranda first saw him at the restaurant of the hotel, when she was eating breakfast, when Michaels sat with an indecisive look in his eyes and then approached her table where she rebuffed him. It was the same wallet he hid Jake's credit card in.

His face was haggard and his hands pale, as if all the blood drained from his body. Michaels handed the wallet to her. "I'm sorry. I was supposed to give this to you when I first saw you at Ground Zero," he said, yet his eyes flashed with defiance, making his words of repentance meaningless.

§

Chapter 37:1

That a woman should lose her heart…

Miranda opened the wallet and there in the little plastic window, Jake stared out at her from his driver's license.

"Jacob wanted you to have this," he said softly and squeezed her arm.

She jerked away from him. "But why did you bring his wallet with you that first day? How did you know I would be at Ground Zero? A bit of a coincidence, don't you think?"

Michaels ran a hand through his hair, looking flustered.

"You said you didn't know where Jake lived, yet all the time you had his wallet. Look. Right here is his address."

He returned her hurt, puzzled stare with a tormented gaze.

"Did you steal Jake's wallet?"

"I may be a lot of things, but a thief is not among them."

Michaels knelt before her, took his handkerchief and wiped her eyes, streaking dry tears across her face. He wet the hankie with his tongue, cleaning the dirt off her cheeks while Miranda hiccupped like a little girl.

"What's this?" she said, pointing to dry, reddish-brown drops on the wallet.

"Blood," he said so quietly, she barely heard him.

She sobbed tears, more like a drizzle that hits the windshield of a car without enough force to really wet the glass.

He appeared even more haggard. Michaels wrung his hands like he was washing them, as if no amount of scrubbing would ever cleanse them. "I want you to know what happened, Miranda. I need you to understand. You have no idea what I'm capable of, the sins I've committed. Even now, you have no idea what my lust has led me to do." He gripped the handles of the chair, staring at the tell-tale signs of blood on Jake's wallet.

"Did you kill my brother?"

He groaned, resting his damp cheek on her shoulder. "I'm not a murderer, Mandy." Yet, he looked remorseful, as if he was responsible for Jake's death.

Frightened by the bleak look haunting his eyes, she backed away from him.

"I did not kill Jake," he said. "Believe me!"

His face looked so woeful that her heart went out to him. Miranda climbed onto his lap, cradling her arms around his neck.

"Sh. It's okay. I do understand," she said, running her fingers through his hair. "I believe it's known as survivor's guilt. As a therapist, I should think you would know this."

"You still think I'm a therapist? Oh, the web we weave," he said with self-mockery.

Miranda was afraid to ask him exactly what he did for a living.

She remembered seeing a burn on his left wrist last night. She lifted his right hand. There on his wrist was another nasty burn where his flesh looked like it had been cooked only yesterday.

He jerked his arm from her and rubbed his wrist.

Poor Michaels has had both wrists burned.

"You mustn't feel guilty because you're a survivor," she said.

"Survivor? That a man should lose his soul."

"And did you, Michaels?"

He blinked his eyes. "Did I what?"

"Did you lose your soul?"

"I thought I had, until I met you."

Michaels leaned back against the chair and closed his eyes.

Miranda brushed back the hair that fell on his forehead, smoothing the strands across his head. Her eyes softened.

Michaels flicked opened his eyes. His gray eyes hardened into steel, and he lifted her off his lap. "There can be nothing between us again. Just stay away from me!"

"Why ever not?" she said, beseeching him with her hands, her voice, her eyes.

Michaels ran his fingers through his hair, pacing across the rug. "It's difficult. Impossible."

"Try me. Tell me what's wrong."

He opened his mouth to speak then clamped his jaw down. Michaels bit down so hard on his cheek, blood dribbled on his lips. He clenched and unclenched his fists.

"If it's your wife," she said.

His fists relaxed. His shoulders slumped as if all the weight of the world pressed down upon him. His head drooped to his chest.

Michaels said nothing, absolutely, godforsaken nothing.

§

Chapter 38:1

And above all, a nation must forgive itself,
For being blind,
For being weak,
For being all too human.

They stared at one another until Ashes crawled from under the bed, yapping, and startling them both.

The spell had been broken. All of it was broken. Michaels turned as if to leave.

Miranda grabbed his arm, clinging to him.

"Forgive me?" he said.

"I forgive you, but why can't you forgive yourself? I thank God you didn't die on 9/11," she said, stroking his cheek.

His face turned the color of a ghastly white. "This can't change things between us, Miranda, though I wish that it could." His eyes were damp. He brought her hand to his lips and kissed her knuckles. "My love, I have to go."

He means to walk away. To leave me here all alone. "Michaels," she cried.

He spun and stared as if memorizing the lines of her face. "Have a good trip back to Los Angeles. Stay safe. I must go," he said, sounding exhausted, as if Michaels tired of this game. His hands hung limp at his sides, yet determination tightened the lines of his face. "I'll meet you later at Ground Zero. I'll wait for you as long as it takes. Forever if need be I'll wait for you at Ground Zero. Come to me."

His words were comforting, yet the look on his face frightened her. Miranda held out a hand to him. "Michaels?" she said, sounding like a mewing kitten that he flung into a well. What she saw in his eyes whirled her around inside his body, making her not care if she ever surfaced. "Michaels!"

He walked back, cupping her cheeks with his hands. He opened his mouth and then snapped it shut. Please understand, his eyes begged her. Michaels closed his eyes, swallowing. He squeezed his eyes tighter, the air rattling in his chest.

Passion smoldered beneath the surface of her eyes. Here was her prince who awakened her to passion, love, longing and to dreaming. Michaels was her tarnished prince.

"Just don't hate me," he whispered.

"I'm confused. Hate you for what?"

"Don't be hasty and do anything you'll regret. Think about all that I've told you."

"And have you done anything you regret?" she said in a tiny voice.

"Not with you, Miranda. Never with you. My Love, I promise I'll be at Ground Zero. Look for me," he said, sounding like he was choking. His eyes, which a moment ago glowed with such passion, burned to gray ashes smoldering around his face.

Look for me, his lips mouthed as he backed away from her. His eyes were still tormented.

Michaels walked away, his back hunched over and his fists buried in his pockets.

She twisted his handkerchief in her hands, and the door closed behind him.

A voice whispered that *you should have followed. You should have run after him and stopped him.*

Miranda jumped from the bed, flung open the door, and ran out of the room.

"Michaels!" she yelled, sprinting through the hallways.

She skidded in front of the elevators. They were all in use.

Miranda opened the door to the stairs and ran down to the lobby.

The elevator doors were open and she sprinted out the front door of the Algonquin.

Once again, she was too late, and Michaels had vanished.

§

Chapter 39:1

9/11 is filled with shadows.

Miranda picked up the bedside lamp, hurling it at the door.

She sat on the bed for nearly an hour, staring at pieces of lamp scattered about the threshold. Like the picture hanging on the wall, she was alone and deserted by her lover. She felt blown about by the wind. Indeed, pieces of her were all over the room.

Her heart pumped weakly on the pillow where his head had laid upon.

Her lungs lay on the rug beside the broken lamp, fluttering for air while she struggled for oxygen on the bed.

Above the slivers of ceramic lamp, her hands pressed against the wooden door that Michaels had touched.

Her conscience was hidden under the bed—*what about Jake?*

The rest of Miranda clung to the yellow, flowered sheet with bloodless fingers. The flowers were the stems keeping her rooted to the bed. A flower dries up and dies even as Miranda was shriveling up and dying.

Flowers represent a rebirth of life. The petals of a flower scatter about the field. The stem hardens and breaks off. A new flower sprouts and takes its place. Thus did the rebirth of Miranda begin with a cold shower helping to clear her mind.

She may not know what was wrong with Michaels, but Miranda was determined to discover his secret, unless he really was a wolf and after one conquest, moved quickly on to his next victim.

She could hear him whisper, I'm not the big bad wolf, Mandy. I'm not a wolf any longer. Not anymore. Not since I met you.

Not a wolf since he met me? Disbelief tinged her thoughts because how can a man change his spots so quickly? Since just five days before?

A few wolves had sniffed around her, but a wolf never affected her before. Miranda always found them laughable. She could see right through wolfish men, just like she'd seen through Michaels, right from the very start when sirens whistled in her ears when she sat beside him on the park bench and his seduction began with his relation to her brother. Jake was the link that had been between them, causing her to lower her guard.

No. This isn't fair. My attraction to Michaels has nothing to do with Jake.

But…what is his relationship to Jake? And why does Michaels look so guilty?

Miranda had been reckless because Michaels was so different than any other man she had known. Most women would throw caution to the wind because of a man like Michaels. He was all charm, the type of wolf any woman would invite into her den, even when she knew he was deliberately seducing her with an expertise that should have warned her. Any woman would welcome him into her den, even aware of what he was, even knowing the danger Michaels posed—to her. After his performance of last night Miranda should feel justified for having wooed Michaels into her den. A woman could be excused for ignoring bells in her head warning what might happen once Michaels left, what was happening to her now. The fact that Michaels hid a secret from Miranda ripped her apart. After all they shared, he did not trust her. Even worse, the suffering she had seen on his face and in his eyes made her afraid for him.

And what of yourself? You should be even more frightened for yourself. What about Jake?

Miranda banged her head against the shower wall, unmindful of shampoo dribbling into her eyes. She refused to even think about a world without Michaels and not being some part of his life.

What if he goes to prison for murdering your brother?

If Miranda allowed herself to think in this manner, she would truly go insane. Michaels had become the catalyst who rocked her world, changed it, turned her life upside down, yet for the very first time, Miranda felt righted. Michaels was her missing link, which is exactly where her dilemma lay, buried in her love for him. She had fallen head over heels and was terminal.

And so, as Miranda air-dried because she was too weary to lift a towel, she stood in the bathroom with her forehead resting against the mirror, trying to understand what could have possibly gone wrong. She struggled to remember every word said.

They had stopped in Central Park at a bronze, horsed statue of King Jagiello of Lithuania and Poland, who defeated the Teutonic Knights of the Cross in 1410.

"Jagiello had four wives and lived to a ripe old age," Michaels had said.

"Was Jake ever in love?"

"How the heck would I know? What is love anyway? I fall in love every time I walk into a bar."

"Most cynics have suffered a broken heart, which is why they are cynical about love," she had said.

He hooted. "Spoken like a true romantic. Love doesn't exist—only the itch a man gets when he wants a woman."

"That's so sexual. What about emotion? How about involvement? What of commitment? Relationships?" she had said with dismay.

"What about them?"

"Weren't your parents in love?"

"Nope, were yours?"

"I think so."

"You don't remember because you were a kid. I've yet to see a marriage where the husband and wife still love each other after seven years. They don't call it the seven year itch for nothing," he had said.

"I believe in a love that can last forever, beyond the grave."

"How sophomoric of you. Okay, Miss Romantic, have you ever been in love?"

"Not really. Not the forever. Not the fairy tale," she had said, smiling wryly.

Michaels had told her he didn't believe in love or commitment or relationships. With a bittersweet feeling, Miranda recalled every gesture and look that passed between them—except one detail was impossible to recall.

Jake. In all of this, Jake is still a shadow.

Michaels had his wallet yet kept it from me. He withheld Jake from me. Jake was the reason we were together in the first place.

A tear flowed down her cheek, dissipating the years, as she once more saw her eleven-year-old brother waving at her, with tears streaming down his face, as he was taken away by Social Services. No one wanted two older children.

Once again, she heard Jake's voice screaming at her, promising that, someday we'll be together again!

Just you and me. Just you and me.

Miranda reached for the hair dryer.

The dryer turned on by itself.

She ducked from the snaking dryer slamming against the wall.

Both sink handles turned on, splashing water.

Miranda grabbed the dryer before it could fall into the sink. She hit the off button and placed the dryer back on the wall.

The toilet flushed by itself.

"That's it, Jake! You're not being funny."

Ashes merely sat, staring at the shower curtain, as if hypnotized.

She tiptoed over to the tub, and yanked the shower curtain open.

No ghost.

Miranda frowned at Ashes. *What an odd little dog.*

The toilet flushed again.

Now what is Jake trying to warn me of? Or maybe he is still alive.

Or perhaps Jake wants his murder avenged and he's angry…

Miranda ran into the bedroom and picked up his wallet, rubbing it against her chest. *Perhaps I should seek out a medium and have a séance. I'll ask Michaels what he thinks, when I see him later at Ground Zero.*

Is that really a good idea, to discover what happened to Jake by asking Michaels' opnion?

While she dressed in jeans and t-shirt, Miranda absentmindedly picked at fruit and sweet rolls delivered to the room.

She sat on the bed, rubbing Jake's wallet between her fingers. The wallet was a soft tri-fold of faded brown leather. The leather smelled burnt.

Miranda never invaded the privacy of a man's wallet before and felt strange doing so, even if it was her brother's wallet.

There was a standard bank credit card accepted all over the world, credit cards for Macy's and Bloomingdale's. A New York Driver's license with a birth-control photo of Jake. Membership card to the gym. Employee identification card for Egghead Revolution. Business card for a pizza delivery takeout place. A stick of gum. Video rental card. Health insurance card. A prophylactic.

Oops, for save sex.

An expired prescription for contact lenses.

A pass, allowing him to work after hours in Building Two of the World Trade Center.

And in the hidden pocket of Jake's wallet was a key.

Miranda was disappointed there were no personal photos.

Stuffed in the money pocket were two twenties, four fives, and three one-dollar bills. Between the dollar bills was a yellowed letter.

She tossed the bills aside and unfolded the letter. A short, typed note was enclosed with the letter.

Miranda set the note aside and opened her eyes wide at the date of the letter—October 13, 1988, nine months after their parents died. A sigh escaped her lips and she hugged the letter to her chest. Her letter. The letter was addressed to her in care of Social Services.

§

Chapter 40:1

Grim reaper, death's keeper—
Fuck off!

Miranda blew her nose with a tissue and read Jake's letter through blinding tears.

Dear Mandy,

My letters just keep on coming back. They won't give me your phone number. They say it is better this way. Who are they to say what's better? I hate adults. I hate this place they put me. My bedroom is a dormitory full of other boys, orphans like me. Only I'm not alone. I have you. I tell them I have family, but they tell me to shut up. They say they'll find a new family for me, but I don't want a new family. Why won't they let me see you? They tell me not to cause any trouble and I won't. I promise I won't. But I have to see you. I'm dying in here. I can't stand it. One day I'll grow up and get out of here, and come get you. You'll see, Mandy. There's the bell calling us to supper.

Write if you get this. I never hear from you. I miss you, Sis.

Love,

Jake

P.S. I promise I'll come back. Somehow, some way, I shall contact you.

With the letter was a short stiff note stamped with the date December 10, 1986. The note read like a form letter.

This is to inform you that an out-of-state family adopted your sister and want no communication with old family ties.

The card had been ripped in two and then taped.

Miranda threw her head on the pillow and cried. It was that bitch who drove her away that first day, the one who kept telling her she knew what was best for children. The woman was a witch who later told her no one wanted her because she was bad.

Miranda placed Jake's wallet against her cheek, rubbing the tell-tale blood stain splattered across the leather. She closed her eyes, feeling dizzy. The room spun around her.

When the spinning stopped, she had been transported to Ground Zero. Flames engulfed the top floors of the Twin Towers. The North Tower had a hole punched in the side of the building about a quarter from the top. Wires snaked out of the holes of the building like sizzling tentacles.

The South Tower had a jumbo jet sticking out of it and the smell of blood filled the air.

Miranda walked toward a slender body lying beneath the South Tower. Clothing rippled across the body, blown about by the wind.

Jake. It was her Jake.

His faded blue jeans had a hole in one scraped knee. His t-shirt was gray from ashes but she could still make out crooked letters spelling out the name—Egghead Revolution. Her brother was just twenty-four years old.

Miranda dropped to her knees, cradling his head on her lap.

Jake.

She stroked his cheek.

A reflection of clouds swirled in his hazel eyes like whipped cream. His lips were blue and there was a slight tilt to his mouth. Once more she could hear him—someday we'll be together again, just you and me, just you and me.

Her shoulders shook with sobs. *Where are you, Jake?*

Terrorists may have taken her brother's life but would never claim his spirit, his soul, the essence that was Jake—his laughter, smiles and tears. Jake had a way of chewing his lip when troubled, a trait inherited by her. His eyes had been big, brown, and filled with life. Jake would remain alive in her memories, all the days of her own life.

The Knight of Death stood in the ruins of Ground Zero, grinning back at her like he had the last laugh.

A chill rippled her spine. *We all must die.*

Jake's blood flowed between her fingers, just like the dried blood on the wallet Miranda rubbed between her fingers, now reddish brown—her brother's blood, Jake's.

She flipped open her eyes, staring at the ceiling. Miranda imagined Jake trapped in the stairwell of the South Tower.

Michaels crept down behind Jake.

He reached out his fingers and picked the wallet from Jake's back pocket. Michaels fled down the stairs, all the while laughing like it was a big joke.

She shook her head. None of it made any sense.

§

Chapter 41:1

And in apartments will echo a hollow sound.

Miranda stood outside Jake's apartment building on West End Avenue that looked like most other apartment buildings. Ashes acted fidgety, scratching at the door and whining.

They entered the building and Ashes knew his way to the elevators, tugging her along. Of course, the dog just followed a strong scent of other pets.

She punched the button for the twenty-seventh floor.

Miranda followed Ashes down the hallway to apartment C, where he scratched at the door and whined. The dog seemed to know where Jake had lived!

*Don't be silly. Ashes just…*She frowned at the dog, unable to think of an explanation. Well, Ashes was always an odd little animal. Perhaps the dog had a strong sixth sense.

Miranda released her breath at the name Balboa written on the little panel beneath the peephole. It was possible Jake had a roommate so she rang the door bell, expecting, hoping Michaels would answer. Being his roommate would explain how Michaels had his wallet. Perhaps Jake forgot it on September 11.

She placed the key from Jake's wallet in the deadbolt, and with baited breath turned the key.

The lock snapped open.

The door to Jake's apartment slowly swung open.

There was a small living room and a tiny kitchen with an open window to the living room, along with a breakfast nook and two stools. The kitchen had white cabinets with pots and pans and dishes. There was one cabinet for food with two cockroaches running around. A stale loaf of bread, three cans of soup, some spices, and a half-full cereal box filled the shelves. Trix had always been Jake's favorite. He used to eat Trix right out of the box, chock full of sugar.

Miranda ignored the cockroaches, reaching her hand into the box and stuffing her mouth with dry cereal. She giggled, remembering the times she and Jake would sneak a box of Trix behind the couch, passing the box back and forth until it was empty.

The shelves of the refrigerator were empty except for condiments, five cans of beer and an opened liter bottle of flat diet-cola. In the freezer top of the refrigerator were two frozen beer mugs.

"So Red Dog's your favorite. Thanks, Jake. Yes, I will have a beer to wash down the Trix." She popped the can top, tossing the aluminum tab over her shoulder. "I'm still messy Mandy, like Jake used to say."

Mussy fussy Missy Mandy. She could hear Jake's voice in her ear, teasing her like when she was a child.

Miranda walked into the living room and rummaged through a stack of music CDs.

"Mm. You like jazz huh? And the Rolling Stones. Well, you can have your jazz but I'll take the ancient Stones any day," she said, inserting a CD into the stereo. The words *I can't get no satisfaction* blared from the speakers.

She swallowed a mouthful of beer.

Miranda picked up a framed picture on top of the television, the place of honor in the living room. The picture was of Jake and her with their parents. She stood between Mama and Daddy, holding their hands. She had pigtails and was giggling.

Jake stood next to Daddy. Jake's arms were folded in front of his chest. He tried his best to look grown up, but his baseball cap was turned sideways on his head.

A long forgotten memory came to her—*Daddy had always used Old Spice Cologne.*

Miranda set the photograph next to her purse so she wouldn't forget to take the picture when she left.

She looked out the living room window. The glass pane covered most of the wall. There were neither curtains nor blinds. Across was the Hudson River and Newark. Jake must have seen this view every day.

I must return tonight and see what the view looks like when the lights of Newark are reflected on the river. I'll sit in the dark. Play some jazz. I'll watch all night so I don't miss a thing. From the West side of Manhattan the stars will be visible. There are no skyscrapers to obstruct the view. Hopefully, there will be a full moon.

A bookcase was on one wall and a few computer books which she ignored. Miranda ran her hands down the titles of the novels. One was particularly worn. She read the jacket of the book, a computer nerd's novel.

Miranda clenched the worn book between her hands. She closed her eyes, running her hands over the book cover like she was a blind person and the book written in Braille.

She could feel Jake's hands holding the book.

Miranda placed the book and photograph in a big shopping bag that was under the kitchen sink.

I'm shopping for memories, keepsakes.

Yet a part of her still refused to believe in Jake's death. After all, there was no body.

Bam! A door slammed.

Miranda waited, expecting Jake to come waltzing into the living room with his arms held open to her. It was all a mistake, he would say.

Ah, no, the slamming door is from the next-door apartment.

Miranda wandered into the bedroom. A calendar poster of the New York Nicks was pinned on one wall. The opposite wall was decorated with posters of playboy flavors of the month.

Men will be men. Obviously, Jake didn't have a steady girlfriend else he never would have gotten away with those beauties on his wall.

On the west wall was a matching window, like in the living room that looked out across the Hudson River. This window was also bare.

Next to the bed on the end table was another photograph, this one in a cheap oak frame. *Jake,* she thought, touching her brother's face.

Just like the child Jake, the adult Jake wore a baseball cap, only backwards on his head. He was laughing with a beer in one hand. He had his arm around the shoulders of a friend. Both men looked drunk. The friend wasn't Michaels.

Maybe Michaels snapped the picture.

In the photograph Jake looked so alive, Miranda expected to hear the front door open and Jake run in and say, Mandy, what took you so long to find me, Sis?

Miranda rifled through his shirts, sniffing each one. Most smelled like fabric softener.

She rubbed a yellow and red ribbed sweater against her cheek before placing the sweater over her head and pushing up the sleeves. The sweater wasn't a bad fit.

Miranda sucked in her breath at the baseball cap on top of the closet. She placed the cap on her head, wearing it backwards like Jake.

In the bathroom everything was neat and the towels folded, just so, across the rods.

In the medicine cabinet was a bottle of aspirin, sinus tablets, over-the-counter allergy pills, and petroleum jelly.

Miranda removed a can of shaving cream from the cabinet, filling up her palm. She lowered her nose to the foam and sniffed. With the sweater rubbing against her skin and the shaving cream in her nose, this was as close as she would ever get to Jake. She felt a little peace—it was comforting to be amongst his things. Miranda hadn't felt this close to her brother since she ceased to dream.

Someday we'll be together again, just you and me.

She turned on the faucet, washing the shaving cream from her hand.

There was a glass on the sink painted with fish matching the bathroom décor. On the floor was a fish rug made in an identical pattern. A shower curtain was hung, made to look like an aquarium.

She rinsed the fish glass, filling it half-way with water. Miranda turned off the faucet and lifted the glass to her mouth.

Just you and me.

She grasped the glass so tightly in her hand, it shattered.

Jake stared back at her from the mirror.

§

Chapter 42:1

Now there is in Manhattan
By the trauma unit
A Wall of Tears,
A Wall of Hope,
A Wall of Prayers,
A Wailing Wall.

Jake looked at Miranda like he felt sorry for her.

Jake, she mouthed, reaching out a hand to the mirror, but Jake faded away.

Her hand was suspended in mid-air, dripping blood into the sink

Quick, she grabbed a small towel and wrapped her hand. Miranda pressed down to stop the bleeding. With a wash rag she cleaned the bathroom sink of her blood.

The towel on her hand was turning red.

Miranda threw the blood-soaked towel into an aqua-marine trash can decorated with plastic fish swimming in the walls. With another small towel she applied pressure to her wound.

Miranda grabbed the photo of Jake by the bed, storing it with her other treasures in the shopping bag.

She stood once more at the window. Miranda never felt so lonely, though she was in a city populated with millions. A crowd murmured from the street below, their voices heard all the way up to the twenty-seventh floor. People were speaking in raised tones in order to be heard above the throng. There was the occasional shout. Taxi cab drivers sat through green lights, honking at people mooing through intersections. Manhattan was a loud-mouthed city that never shut up.

Jake's apartment got so quiet, she could have heard a pin drop.

The CD player buzzed.

Miranda supposed she should turn it off, and then a song began playing that was hers and Jake's favorite the year their parents died—R.E.M.'s *Losing My Religion.*

She mouthed the lyrics; *I thought that I heard you laughing. I thought that I heard you sing. I think I thought I saw you try. But that was just a dream. Try. Cry! Why? Try? That was just a dream. Just a dream. Just a dream. Dream…*

Miranda slid to the floor, hugging Ashes and crying into his fur. If not for the little dog, she might jump out the window.

Finally, she calmed down; taking comfort in the fact that Jake's death went very quickly for him, yet he was still very much with her—the song that just played and all the other signs.

She hadn't noticed the picture on the entertainment center.

Jake is holding a dog. Ashes! The dog is Ashes! Jake's dog.

She held Ashes in front of her by his front legs, swinging her head between the dog and the picture. The resemblance was uncanny, the markings and coloring identical. "You're Jake's dog. How did you find me at Ground Zero?"

Ashes yapped and she squeezed him tightly, crying and laughing at the same time.

At least, Miranda wanted to believe in miracles and that Ashes might be Jake's dog. There were a lot of Shih Tzus in New York City.

Michaels had said, some of the offices of the Twin Towers allowed employees to take their pets to work.

Ashes knew which apartment belonged to Jake. She kissed the dog on his wet nose. "You are a miracle, Ashes, and somehow you found me at Ground Zero."

Miranda grabbed the CD from the player and the picture of Ashes and Jake. She shoved them in baggies, and dropped the CD and photo in her bag of treasures. She locked the front door behind her.

Miranda walked down the stairs, her shoes echoing so it sounded like someone was walking with her.

Several times, she stopped.

There was a noise of shoes running down the stairs behind her.

She twirled.

No one was there.

"Jake," she whispered.

The stairwell was eerily quiet—the smell of Old Spice clung to the railing.

Daddy had worn Old Spice Cologne. Oh, God, is my father haunting me, too?

The stairs creaked and something brushed against her shoulders.

The hair rose on the back of her neck.

She ran down the stairs.

Miranda felt a strong sense of foreboding when she reached the bottom. She practically flew out the door of the building. "Can you get me a cab?" she asked the doorman. She was breathless and her voice shaky. Her lungs hurt, not from running but from fear. If her father was a ghost haunting her, why would she be so afraid?

"You should get to a hospital, Miss," the doorman said, noting the blood-soaked towel around her hand.

"Yes, I suppose so." It wouldn't do to faint from loss of blood at Ground Zero. *Michaels promised to meet me there.*

A taxi came to a halt, and the doorman held the door open for her. "Take this young lady to the nearest hospital," he instructed.

The cab driver nodded his head.

Miranda pulled herself together and requested he drive her to the pizza place that was on the takeout card she found in Jake's apartment.

She shared a slice of Meat Lover's Delight with Ashes while the cab went clear across Manhattan to the east side of the city to First Avenue. The cabbie then drove south, thirty blocks to Twenty-Eighth Street.

Miranda didn't tip the driver. She could not believe this hospital was the closest from the northwest side of the city. She, also, bled on his back seat.

Serves him right. Creep.

The hospital may not have been the closest, but Miranda wondered if it was the biggest in the city. Bellevue Hospital stretched for two blocks along the East River.

A sign claimed that Bellevue had healed the city since 1794.

Miranda handed one of the emergency staff her medical insurance card, filled out the necessary forms and waited for an hour to see a doctor.

A nurse shepherded her to a bed, ordering Miranda to put on a hospital gown. The nurse then drew the curtains around her cubicle.

There was a sink in the room and Miranda washed the bloodstain from Jake's sweater.

She sat on the bed, waiting and wondering why the heck she had to undress when the wound was on her hand.

Finally, a doctor flung open the curtain encircling her bed. "How did you cut your hand?" he said.

"My brother, even as children Jake played too rough. See this scar on my forehead. Jake. He threw a towel at me, and I turned my head, hitting my forehead against the bed. Another time, it was a shovel that Jake hit the back of my head with. Oh, he didn't mean to. Jake wasn't like that at all. He was just throwing dirt at me. It was an accident. Boys will be boys."

"Well, tell your brother to be more careful," the doctor said, examining her chart.

"I will. Did you get many 9/11survivors at Bellevue?"

"We have the biggest trauma center in Manhattan," the doctor said in a voice bouncing off the sterile walls of the noisy emergency ward. "Extra staff was called in to help. Another burn unit was put together. But we all waited. We stood around feeling useless, helpless, hopeless, and gutless. The morgue was busier than we were." The doctor had a haunted look in his eyes. He shuffled with his papers, clicking his teeth together.

"Oh," she said, not knowing what else to say. Miranda could have told him she lost her brother when the towers fell, the brother who cut her hand earlier. The brother whose body was never found. The brother whose ghost she kept seeing. But she didn't want the doctor's pity, nor did Miranda want him to prescribe antidepressants or anxiety medication. He might lock her up. Bellevue once had an insane asylum.

A nurse recited release instructions for her wound.

Miranda walked out of Bellevue with twelve stitches on her right hand.

Just a little more to the right and the glass might have sliced my wrist. I could have bled to death.

She sobered at the hoards of photographs and small posters on the outside walls of Bellevue. There was a banner strung across that read, WALL OF PRAYERS. Here families and friends of the missing posted pictures near the entrance to the hospital, just in case. Over the two weeks since the tragedy, the Wall of Prayers turned into a makeshift, open-aired, Missing Persons Bureau. The Wall of Prayers began as a sea of missing faces. After two weeks of silence from the rubble of ground Zero, the Wall of Prayers was a vast ocean of hopelessness.

The wall put a face to the missing—men and women cut down in the prime of life. The victims looked so full of life;

Miranda felt that if she touched their photos, their skin would be as warm as their eyes and their hair as soft as their smiles.

How could so many possibly be dead?

Smiling, laughing faces stared back at her. They all looked so friendly, like people she would like to have known. There were young men and women, and others old enough to retire. Black. Oriental. White. Hispanic. All colors were represented. Some held babies. Others carried children on their shoulders. Another hugged a dog to his chest. One man blew out candles on a birthday cake—birthdays that would never be celebrated again.

Not many bodies had yet been recovered, if they ever would. Just a little over a hundred so far. Thousands of others looked out from the Wall of Prayers.

The missing all had a name and vital statistics, a heartbeat, brain, and a soul.

There was a murmuring of voices around the Wall of Prayers, coming from the mingling crowd.

Sara and I always played tennis. She had this way of holding her racket.

Tom was a closet fan of the Dallas Cowboys, just like you.

Jim knew everything there was to know about cars. If he was here right now, I could give him a call and he'd come over and help you start that wreck of yours.

Melanie was real smart. She was studying for her degree. She's majoring in art too. I'm surprised you never ran into her on campus.

Charlie is coaching his son's hockey team. Next year, your son would've been on his team. I'm sure he would've welcomed an assistant coach like you.

Remember that policeman who stopped us a few months ago? He was such a nice guy. He only gave us a warning, remember?

That fireman who lives in the building across the street from us. The guy who always waves. Do you remember his name? He introduced himself when we first moved here, but I'm so hard with names. That face under that red helmet though, I'll never forget that face.

His roaring laughter.

The way his eyes crinkled when amused.

She had the most gorgeous walk, didn't she? Really sexy.

The way he used to spit, it was so cool.

She was always cracking her gum. It annoyed the hell out of me. If she was only here, I'd buy her a year's supply of gum. She must have tasted like bubble gum.

He always blinked his right eye three times when he had a good hand, but he thought he had a poker face so he'd bet big. Then he'd always lose, dumb jerk.

She was from the Bronx. Her accent was so thick; she used to make people laugh just by talking. We told her she should be a comedian. She said she'd think about it. You know, there are those nights at the comedy clubs when you can try out. I wish...

Man, could he tie one on. And you'd never know it. He could walk a straight line from here to Kingdom Come and fool even Him.

She used to sing in choir and throw everyone off key. They only let her stay 'cause she was so nice.

He used to bring in donuts to the office every time the Yankees won.

She always cleaned the coffee pots, even though she hated coffee. She was a neat freak, I guess, but I don't really know. I should have taken the time to get to know her better.

He was the janitor on our floor, and I never even told him good morning.

She always smelled so good, like bubble bath. I wonder what perfume she used. Or toilet water. Yeah. Toilet water was more her style. Not the Frenchy perfume type. She wasn't stuck up at all. I wish I'd had the courage to ask her out.

He had these big muscles. He used to work out all the time. He flexed his arm once, and let me touch the bulging lump. He was so strong. He of all people should have gotten out.

And on and on and on.

Miranda dragged her feet, scanning the photographs on the Wall of Prayers, looking for Jake. Maybe the friend in the photograph she had in her shopping bag put up Jake's picture. Perhaps Michaels posted her brother's photo. She would ask him at their meeting this afternoon at Ground Zero.

I'm becoming a believer. My fortune at the Chinese restaurant was right. It read: You will hear from someone you have not seen in a long time.

I promise I'll come back. Somehow, some way, I shall contact you—it had taken thirteen years, but Jake kept his promise.

All is not always what it seems.

He who manipulates fate gets what he deserves.

This picture. This picture. Her eyes froze on a photograph on the Wall of Prayers. *This face. His face.*

A smiling, golden man with sparkling gray eyes stared out at her from the Wall of Prayers. Below the picture were the words:

MISSING

CHRISTOPHER (CHRIS) MICHAELS

Height 6'2" Weight 175 pounds
Dark blonde hair, gray eyes
Wearing an NYU graduation ring and gold watch
Class of '93
Last seen: 2 World Trade Center, 42nd Floor
September 11, 2001

If you have any information, please contact...

The date of the posting was September 13, two days after the tragedy.

§

Chapter 43:1

And parents will cry for their children.

Miranda stared with disbelief at Michaels' missing poster on the Wall of Prayers.

It must be difficult to find a picture amongst so many. It was no coincidence I stumbled upon his photo, as if it beckoned me.

Michaels had said—do you really think it is a coincidence that out of all the thousands mourning at Ground Zero, it happened to be me you bumped into?

Why would his picture be with the missing, two days after the tragedy? Perhaps friends thought Michaels was missing and put up his photograph. In the confusion, a lot of people were thought to be missing who later turned up okay.

Nevertheless, it was eerie seeing his photo among the missing. Miranda intended to tell Michaels she found him on the Wall of Prayers, and that he should get the word out to all who know him that he is alive and well.

In the meantime, she ripped his poster from the Wall of Prayers.

Miranda pulled out her cell phone from her purse and dialed the contact information listed on the poster.

"Michaels' residence," a feminine voice answered on the other end of the phone line.

So it was family who posted his picture. She frowned at who the other woman might be.

"My name is Miranda Balboa," she told the woman in a clipped business-like voice. "I'm a friend of Michaels, Chris...Christopher's. His picture is posted at the Wall of Prayers with the missing."

There was a heartfelt sigh at the other end of the line, followed by a weary voice. "We forgot to take down the pictures we posted."

Miranda was about to assure the woman that she had removed the poster.

"What with the funeral and all," the woman said.

"The funeral?"

"Chris is no longer missing. Some remains were recovered from the ruins of the World Trade Center. We buried him a week ago at Calvary Cemetery," the woman said in a strangled voice.

"Did I dial the right number?" Miranda asked in a dazed voice. She repeated the phone number on the missing poster.

There was a silence at the other end of the line followed by heavy breathing.

"Please, I'm just trying to figure out…," Miranda said.

"You dialed correctly. Are you a friend?" the woman said.

"Christopher can't be dead. You must have buried the wrong man. I just saw him this morning. I wanted to tell you that he's no longer missing. I don't know why he hasn't contacted you."

"My husband put up that poster of our son before his body was recovered. He was burned, but DNA proved beyond a doubt that it was Chris. He wore a graduation ring on his finger with his name engraved around the inside of the ring, Chris Michaels. The year he graduated from NYU, 1993, was engraved next to the stone. We chose to bury him with his ring on. Please. Leave us alone. Can't you see what you're doing?"

An angry man came on the line. "You're upsetting my wife."

"But there must be a mistake. You didn't bury the Christopher Michaels who you claim to be missing on the poster. You..."

"If you call here again, I'll call the police."

Click.

Miranda had a sick feeling in her stomach. She closed her eyes. *Not Michaels. This means that he is...That he...*

Michaels can't be dead! He was just with me this morning. I've seen him every day. Spent time with him. Ate with him. Drank with him. Laughed with him. Made love with him. His parents are mistaken. Their son was just here. He gave me Jake's wallet. Michaels couldn't be buried at Calvary Cemetery.

And what about Jake's wallet? How did Michaels get Jake's wallet?

And then there was the DNA test.

Technology makes mistakes. DNA tests are made by men in white lab coats.

I know Michaels is alive. What I don't understand is why Michaels hasn't contacted his family.

Miranda hailed a taxi, and the driver told her Calvary Cemetery was in Flushing, about ten or fifteen minutes away.

In the back of the cab, Miranda held onto Ashes like the dog was a lifeline. "Well, you must be a survivor, too," she whispered in the dog's ear. "Why would Michaels hide from his family?"

She couldn't think of him as Chris, a nickname reserved for friends and family.

And what am I?

Someone he met after he died and made love to as a ghost?

Miranda shook her head at such a preposterous notion.

Nor could she ever think of Michaels as Christopher. She was too used to thinking of him as simply Michaels. The name suited him far more than stuffy Christopher did.

Michaels was never missing, dead or buried.

Was he even at his office when the tragedy happened, or was he running late that day like a few lucky others?

Miranda couldn't help but wonder if Michaels was involved in a life insurance scam.

Perhaps, he is running away from a mountain of debt he can't surmount.

In the meantime, Michaels must have found Jake's wallet in the rubble of Ground Zero.

Maybe he is adventurous.

Or planning to commit a crime.

It could be Michaels hid a criminal background and wanted to make a fresh start.

Or he was angry with his family. Michaels ducked out of St. Patrick's as soon as he noticed his family in line to take Communion.

And there is the mystery woman at Macy's, Michaels' so-called sister. Maybe he is running away from a bad marriage—he hid from the woman between aisles of merchandise.

I can't believe I was stupid enough to become involved with a married man, an evil I always swore to avoid. Because of Jake, I threw all caution to the wind.

No. This isn't right. Be truthful. I can't help what I feel for Michaels. Something stronger seemed to be pulling me towards him. I never really gave a damn if Michaels is married, she thought, rubbing her forehead.

Children?

Miranda thought about this and then sighed with relief. *No, he had said, children would have been nice, implying there aren't any. Michaels, also, said he was fixed so sterile, which is odd considering his young age. Maybe his wife doesn't want kids. Oh, well, it doesn't matter. Nothing stops me from feeling the way I do. Any salvation I may have had was lost last night when he made love to me.*

Miranda wasn't off the hook yet though. She sat at a red light with a frown wrinkling her brow. There were a lot of details lacking when it came to Michaels. He was cocky, arrogant, conceited and a real smart ass.

Let's see. What else? Oh yeah. He's probably married. How can I possibly love him? But love is in spite of, and unconditional surrender.

But then again, maybe Michaels isn't married. He suffers from just plain vanilla amnesia. He said he hit his head and has blackouts.

Michaels knows who he is. He always knew.

He pointed out where his apartment is and where his parents live.

Miranda sucked in her breath at her old fear. *Perhaps he has a brain tumor and is dying.*

She recalled his words in the cab: I have to go back.

Did Michaels have to go back to the hospital where he escaped from?

Get serious. Dressed as he was.

Perhaps, he ripped his clothes off some doctor. Maybe he escaped from an insane asylum.

Half the time, Michaels looked like he was homeless.

"Calvary Cemetery," the cabbie said and yanked the taxi over to the curb.

§

Chapter 44:1

And cemeteries will be missing thousands.

The cemetery was lush green lawn, but Ashes refused to get out of the cab. "Well, I don't blame you, Boy. I'm unsure that I should be here, except that I have to see with my own eyes," Miranda said.

She didn't have to check the gravesite directory. Miranda walked towards a gravestone upon which sat a white dove. The bird flew away headed in the direction of ...

She rubbed her eyes with her fists. The grave confirmed what the woman on the phone said. On the headstone was an epitaph to the man she spent the last week with:

Christopher Brian Michaels
Beloved son and brother
His smile was infectious.
His strength unyielding.
Born into this world on November 13, 1970
Struck down by a senseless act of terrorism September 11, 2001
His spirit has soared beyond the smoldering ruins.
But take comfort. Chris has not left us.
He will forever live on in our hearts.
Chris will always be our hero.

Surely, there is a mix-up. The body of the imposter buried beneath this mound of earth was burned beyond recognition. The DNA test had to be flawed.

Michaels is alive! Miranda was sure of it. Yet, seeing his name in a graveyard with flowers wilting on a fresh grave was eerie. The cemetery was surreal and spooky, like a horror film with her playing the female lead.

She shouldn't have come here.

Miranda once more read the name, Christopher Brian Michaels, engraved on the marble and then looked at the picture of the missing man she clutched in her hand, Christopher (Chris) Michaels.

He never said he had been missing.

Michaels must have known they were looking for him.

He should have contacted his family. It's been two weeks.

In a city where both Michaels and his parents live, he seemed like a stray with nowhere to go. He claimed to have spent all night outside her apartment building.

He hid from his sister or wife at Macy's, instead of revealing himself and the fact that he was alive and survived the attack.

Michaels hid from the owner of his dog, probably his father.

He never had any money on him.

Her legs were like jelly, and Miranda was barely able to navigate back to the taxi.

Get control of yourself, Miranda. The cabbie and Ashes are looking at you.

§

Chapter 45:1

And education was used not to teach but to destroy with a plane.

Miranda walked across the campus of NYU located in the heart of Greenwich Village.

She ordered Ashes to wait outside of the Student Services Center. At the Office of the University Registrar was an information desk. A woman with a name tag of Maria stitched across her blouse looked up from filing her nails. She raised an eyebrow and cracked her gum.

"Where can I look up the names of graduates?" Miranda said.

"Who you lookin' for?"

"Is there more than one Christopher Brian Michaels who graduated in the year 1993, or Chris Michaels?"

And, oh by the way, can you tell me if there are two or more former students named Christopher Michaels, do they have matching DNA? Perhaps Michaels was cloned. Maybe NYU has a cloning program.

Insanity. Keep it cool. Don't lose your head.

Lord knows, you've already lost your heart to a dead man.

Shut up.

Miranda straightened her hair with shaky fingers while the woman punched the keys of her computer.

"Mm," the woman said, like a grave mystery flickered across her monitor. "There is only one graduated that year. In fact there is only one Christopher Brian Michaels ever graduated NYU."

"How about Chris Michaels or Christopher Michaels?"

"Only one graduated 1993."

Miranda winced. "Is there a bathroom around here?"

"Bathroom's behind me," Maria grunted, twisting her belly and pointing out the direction. She clucked her tongue against the roof of her mouth. "You all right? Honey, you look like you've seen a ghost. Take the first left before the elevators. You'll run right into the bathrooms." The phone rang and she picked up the receiver.

Miranda relieved herself and then washed her hands. She cupped water from the faucet and drank. She sprinkled more water on her face and dried with a paper towel.

The water failed to refresh her.

You look like you've seen a ghost; Michaels had told her when she first ran into him.

"You look like you are a ghost," she said, throwing the paper towel at her image.

Miranda rested her forehead against the glass and tapped the mirror with her fingernails. She struggled to gain control of her emotions. It didn't help that it seemed these past days some outside force was leading her here, to this place and this moment.

Miranda couldn't get that damn graduation ring out of her mind.

Last night, she glanced down at his finger, noticing the year 1993 engraved along one side. The letters NYU were engraved along the other side of the ring. He told her he graduated from NYU.

Miranda had stood at Ground Zero and seen Jake's ghost, several times.

Did I imagine Michaels then? Have I spent the last days at Ground Zero dreaming of him? I wanted to hear from Jake so badly that I would make up...that I would…Am I insane?

The hankie! She had his handkerchief in her jacket pocket.

Miranda fanned open the square of linen, rubbing the tell-tale letters CBM monogrammed across one corner with black thread.

All is not always what it seems.

He who manipulates fate gets what he deserves.

She clutched his handkerchief, her nails cutting into her palm. *Surely, Michaels is alive! There has got to be an explanation.*

Miranda slammed the bathroom door. She had to replace this helpless feeling.

"What the hell is going on, Michaels?" she said aloud in front of the elevator.

The elevator doors opened, and she reached out a finger to push the lobby button.

Which room is yours, he had asked

She covered her face with her hands, feeling in the middle of a nervous breakdown. A nightmare was unfolding. Perhaps there were more horrors to come.

Get control of yourself!

The elevator doors snapped shut. Miranda was trapped by memories, glorious remembrances. Only last night, Michaels grabbed her and kissed her in an elevator. If she closed her eyes, Miranda could still feel his lips, his body pressing against her. He held her arm behind her back, pushing her against the wall of the elevator and grinding into her.

She had wrapped her thighs around his waist.

She could still feel Michaels…

The elevator bell rang. The doors opened and Miranda held her breath, expecting to see the hallway of the Algonquin.

She walked across the NYU campus.

No one saw her. Miranda was invisible.

Maybe I'm dead, too.

§

Chapter 46:1

The word became flesh.
And the word lived among us.
And the word was terror.

Miranda pushed open the main door of the Times Square Building where the *New York Times* newspaper was located. Presses worked at maximum output, unable to keep up with a story so big; there weren't enough front pages of the world's newspapers to contain it. The walls smelled of ink. The air tingled with the fear of tomorrow's news and the excitement of a late-breaking story.

News reporters were still reeling from shock that this happened here in America. Many of these reporters had witnessed devastation of war from front lines around the world. The destruction of the WTC was the news story of all centuries. Indeed, there was an aura surrounding the Times Square Building of anticipation and dread of what would happen next.

From the information desk Miranda discovered where the archives were. "Excuse me," she said to a bald employee.

"Huh?" The man rattled his newspaper.

"Where are the newspapers from this month?"

"Dates are all there to your right."

The newspapers were hanging, clipped to binders. Miranda slid the binders across the railing, stopping at the week of September 11. She removed the binder, carrying the newspapers over to a table and sat down.

With a sick feeling, she navigated through obituaries filled with names of victims of the attack, including police officers and firemen. She skimmed her fingers down the obituaries of September 16. Her heart skipped a beat at the name Michaels printed in big bold letters.

Miranda waited for her heart to begin beating again. Then she read the obituary:

Christopher (Chris) Brian Michaels was killed at the attack of the WTC on September 11. He was the son of Roy and Elizabeth Michaels of New York City. He is also survived by a brother, Dr. Lyle Michaels of New York City and a sister, Michelle Michaels Bryant, wife of John Bryant of Westchester, New York.

Miranda placed a hand over her mouth. She felt like throwing up as she recalled not believing Michaels about his sister.

She nervously placed her hair behind her ear. The words of the paper were a blur. She wiped her eyes with the backs of her hands. It was disarming to read about his death. Of course Miranda didn't believe Michaels was dead, but it was upsetting all the same.

She took a deep breath and continued reading.

Chris Michaels was born and raised in the city. He graduated in 1993 from NYU with honors. Since 1997, Chris was employed at the WTC by the firm of Lansing and Lansing Trading House.

A memorial service will be held at St. Patrick's Cathedral on September 17th at seven o'clock in the evening. Funeral services are at ten a.m. on September 18th at Calvary Cemetery in Flushing. See A-20.

Miranda shook her head and mewed. His fingerprints were all over her body. The taste of his lips was on her mouth.

She sniffed the sleeve of her jacket and smelled Michaels. The odor of peaches drifted up through her nasal passages.

She could still hear his husky voice vibrate with emotion—sh, we've plenty of time.

In the obituary there was no mention of a widow. *The secret he hid from me.* She laughed hysterically. *So he isn't married. Michaels is just dead.*

Her face paled as she recalled that last night, in bed, Michaels had not been cold, like a dead man, but warm and very much alive.

Just don't hate me, he had pleaded.

It was crazy to even think of Michaels being a ghost. Miranda thought, *Michaels can't be dead! They buried the wrong man, a man burned beyond recognition. The DNA—science doesn't make mistakes.*

Ah, but humans take scientific tests and read the results. Humans do err, all the time. The collapse of the Twin Towers is proof of that. No one ever thought a commercial plane could be made into a bomb. The fact that the towers would collapse due to a plane hitting them at full speed was thought to be impossible before 9/11.

Michaels has amnesia. That's why he hasn't gotten in touch with his family.

But Michaels recognized his sister at Macy's and hid from her. He didn't expose himself because he is dead.

Miranda felt like screaming as she spilled the contents of her purse on the table. She sorted through the mess of a wallet. Can of mace. Pen. Notepad. Pack of gum. Sunglasses case. Calculator. Lotion. Bank statement. Keys. Employee badge. Hotel key. Phone bill. Hairbrush. Blush. Comb. Lipstick. Eyebrow brush. Penlight.

Have I lost my mind? Where is it?

She lifted her checkbook and breathed a sigh of relief because beneath the checkbook was Jake's wallet. Inside the wallet was an envelope, yellowed with age. She opened the envelope and inside was Jake's letter.

There was the mystery of Michael's class ring. His mother told her, we chose to bury him with his ring on. *Michaels was wearing an NYU ring last night. Something doesn't add up.*

His lied to both his family and me.

He is hiding for some reason.

"Just what the hell are you up to, Michaels?"

My God! Wait a minute. There is a mistake.

§

Chapter 47:1

Amongst the decay, hope will prevail.

Miranda reread a line of the obituary: Since 1998 Chris Michaels was employed at the WTC by the firm of Lansing and Lansing Trading House.

She pulled out her cell phone and dialed the number of Egghead Revolution.

"Do you have an employee named Christopher Michaels who worked for you at the World Trade Center? Who's missing, or dead, or alive?"

"Nope. Sorry."

"Chris Michaels?"

"Nope."

"Brian Michaels?"

"No Michaels at all. Never had a Michaels at Egghead Revolution. I've been here since the company got its seed money."

Miranda hung up the phone, quickly dialed information and asked for Lansing and Lansing Trading House.

But the office perished on 9/11, along with corporate America's naiveté.

Nevertheless, a voice answered, "Lansing and Lansing."

"I thought you were closed down since the World Trade Center…"

"This is the Upper Eastside Office. Most of our employees made it out."

"Christopher Michaels?"

The man cleared his throat. "Christopher died on September 11. His remains have been recovered. I believe his funeral was last week."

Miranda pressed the end button of her cellular phone, cutting off the lies.

Her fingers shook so badly she barely managed to turn the newspaper to page A-20.

Miranda shook her head in disbelief at two photographs, side by side—Michaels and her brother Jake.

The article was a tale of heroism, not a unique circumstance given the tragedy of September 11, a day filled with heroes. The hero this newspaper article trumpeted was one Jacob Balboa.

Jacob had worked for Egghead Revolution, a technical startup with enough venture capital backing to afford a midtown office and office space at the World Trade Center's South Tower. According to co-workers, Jacob stayed behind in the South Tower to help a man named Chris Michaels. A heavy mass of debris had fallen on Michaels' leg, and he couldn't move. Jacob and another co-worker tried to remove the mass but were unsuccessful. In the meantime, Michaels passed out.

Jacob opted to stay with Michaels until help arrived. The co-worker, who tried to help Jacob lift the debris from Michaels' leg, agreed to send for help as soon as he got out of the tower. Jacob would stay behind and make sure that whoever arrived to help Michaels would be able to find the now unconscious man.

The co-worker told a fireman about the two men trapped in the tower and what floor they were on, along with their location.

The fireman entered the South Tower, along with several other firemen.

Shortly thereafter, the South Tower collapsed.

If not for Christopher Michaels, Jacob Balboa would be alive, but he chose to stay behind in the doomed building and help a stranger, a man who worked on another floor for a different company. The two strangers died together the story went on to say in conclusion.

At Tavern on the Green, Michaels slammed his glass down in anger, shattering the glass to splinters—your brother could have saved himself but chose to stay behind to help an injured man who was doomed, a stranger.

A stranger? Did I ever really know Michaels?

Miranda focused on his picture in the paper. She blinked at his arms, the same arms that caressed her. His hands had been all over her body, worshipping her, just last night.

His voice had whispered in her ear, I'm sorry.

Sorry for what? Lying to me?

The obituary told the truth about where he worked, proving Michaels was guilty of lying. Michaels took advantage of her weakness, even last night.

Especially last night.

Miranda didn't want to think about last night. The article and the lies was enough to deal with. Maybe Michaels was just an adventurous bastard, a man whose word was meaningless.

Michaels said him and Jake both worked together. He lied about them being best friends.

Was it a simple chance of fate that she and Michaels should meet, like Michaels implied?

Or was it?

Michaels had Jake's wallet and the key to Jake's apartment, along with the address. He may have been in his apartment and recognized me from the family portrait. I did have Jake's missing poster at Ground Zero. Michaels may have looked over my shoulder.

Do you really think it is a coincidence that out of all the thousands mourning at Ground Zero, it happened to be me you bumped into, he had said.

Miranda fished from her own wallet the picture of her and Michaels taken at the Four Joys, just yesterday. There was no mistake. The man in both photographs, the person in the *New*

York Times story and the man sitting beside her at a restaurant in Chinatown was the same man she spent the last week with.

The proof was here—Michaels' hankie, the photo taken at the Four Joys, and Jake's wallet. This was the evidence that made her sane, irrefutable proof that Michaels is alive.

There has to be a mistake. Somehow Michaels got out of the South Tower before the building fell.

Even though he was unconscious?

Even though he was trapped by heavy debris?

Even after he told you himself how Jake died?

My brother is dead because of Michaels. Is it any wonder Michaels looked guilty when I asked him if he killed Jake?

Miranda stared at his picture in the *New York Times.*

Those same full lips kissed her just this morning in her room. Miranda touched her lips and closed her eyes. Even now she could feel his mouth on hers. Indeed, her lips were still swollen from the night before.

Minutes seemed to pass into hours when Miranda finally wiped her eyes with her sleeve. With swollen lids she examined his picture more closely.

Michaels stared back at her from a black and white photo. His blonde hair was cut raggedy to his shoulders. He looked very somber, dressed in a suit.

Michaels' eyes seemed to soften in that picture—forever if need be, I'll wait for you at Ground Zero, Miranda. Come to me.

She dropped his obituary into her purse.

§

Chapter 48:1

And the fallen will leave behind mementos.

"Ground Zero," she told the cab driver

The cabbie must have sensed the urgency in her voice. He floored the gas pedal.

Jake wrote the letters DAED on my hotel window. Backwards, the letters are the word DEAD. Jake was warning me about Michaels, she thought. Michaels own dog didn't even know him. His being a ghost would explain his reluctance to see his sister and his hiding from his father.

Miranda tried to breathe normally and not hyperventilate. That day in Central Park, she and Michaels wandered over to her favorite statue. Preserved in bronze was the lost Alice in Wonderland sitting atop a mushroom. The March Hare stood beside the mushroom with his clock open.

How could the week have fallen through the cracks of time? For tomorrow only promises to come and the minutes of yesterday are scattered about by the wind until only fragments of a memory remain. Time is an oak with leaves falling, while winter lurks in the shadows until the tree is bare.

Miranda felt like Alice who fell down a rabbit hole. It seemed her life had fallen through the cracks of time.

She closed her eyes, concentrating on his last words—My Love, I promise I'll be at Ground Zero. Look for me.

Miranda tipped the taxi driver handsomely for getting her to Ground Zero so fast.

She was pushed to the front of the crowd and dropped to her knees. She bowed her head, her face hidden behind a curtain of hair. Miranda waved a small, American flag someone shoved at her. A large US flag was draped over a particularly big piece of the

North Tower, like a burial shroud. The makeshift flagpole was actually the 360-foot antenna that once topped the North Tower and shot from the roof like a javelin when the building collapsed. Workers recovered the large flag in the debris and duct taped it to a piece of wood, mounting it on the pseudo-flagpole that was once the WTC communications antenna. The flagpole was angled at forty-five degrees rather than perpendicular.

Miranda bowed her head and said a prayer for the men and women who died here.

This is where she had begun, simmering with emotion at the spaghetti of twisted metal that had once been the Twin Towers. Miranda was still brimming with hurt because this time, she held in her hands an obituary claiming Christopher Michaels was killed on September 11th.

Do you really think it is a coincidence that out of all the thousands mourning at Ground Zero it happened to be me you bumped into, he had said.

Miranda now suspected Michaels had searched for her in the crowd and bumped into her.

"Why isn't Michaels here?" she said, hugging Ashes in her arms so tightly, the dog whined. She wiped her tears on his dirty neck before setting Jake's dog on the ground.

Ashes cowered before the rubble and the smell of smoke still coming from Ground Zero.

Miranda swallowed the lump in her throat, wondering about how Michaels came to possess another man's wallet. No man ever surrendered his wallet freely to another.

Michaels lied about working with Jake. No telling what other lies he spun in his deceitful web.

Stop it, Miranda. Just stop it. Quit judging him. You don't have all the facts, she thought, rubbing her neck and eyeing the obituary. *He lied to me but it doesn't change the way I feel about him*

My Love, I promise I'll be there at ground zero, he had said.

There was no sign of Michaels.

Miranda had so many questions. She sensed from the beginning there was something odd about Michaels, but she never doubted his character and believed him to be a man of principle. She desperately needed to give Michaels the benefit of the doubt.

Once she had a chance to speak with him, they would both laugh about the misunderstanding.

Among the dull twisted metal something flashed in the sun. Miranda lifted her arms to ward off the blinding light. Blinking her eyes against the brightness, she picked up a ring. It was a class ring from NYU and the graduation class of 1993.

Her hair rose on the back of her neck when she read the name Chris Michaels engraved on the interior of the band of gold. Michaels' graduation ring was not in a grave on the finger of an imposter but here at the ruins of the Twin Towers.

Calm down! Think! Michaels is just shell shocked. Anyone who has gone through his ordeal must be suffering from Post Traumatic Stress Syndrome. This might explain him allowing his family to bury the wrong man. Michaels has survivor's guilt—since the ones who died no longer have a family, neither does he.

Miranda placed his ring on her finger.

I hope I'm not too late, and Michaels hasn't given up on me.

§

Chapter 49:1

It is said that if one dies a violent death,
His ghost will haunt the place that holds his name.

A rollercoaster of emotions twisted her insides—an anguish so devouring, Miranda didn't think she could bear it. Michaels left her his ring, which meant that he wasn't coming.

"But Michaels promised to wait for me here at Ground Zero!"

The little dog she found lost among the rubble of the WTC, Jake's dog, ran between her legs, nearly making her lose her balance. Ashes ran under the yellow tape and leaped into the arms of a man who materialized in the fog.

It was Michaels who hugged the dog, as though he lost an old friend.

Miranda could see right through Michaels, to the twisted ruins of the WTC.

Their eyes locked. His beautiful gray eyes, swimming with emotion.

Her own eyes drowned in tears.

His face looked haggard, his shoulders slumped in defeat. Just like before, his expression was desolate. Still, there was an aura of defiance about him.

Michaels stretched out his hand to her, as though he would touch her once again.

Even now.

Across the worlds separating them.

Miranda quivered with raw emotion. She felt what Michaels felt. Their minds melded. Their hearts beat as one.

Miranda could not move any closer, could not breech the gulf parting them.

She screamed—Michaels was fading yet, she could feel him pulling her closer.

She heard his deep, masculine voice that always sounded as if it came from inside the Lincoln Tunnel, only now she knew his voice came from under the rubble of Ground Zero.

—Mandy.

"Michaels, please come back to me."

He hung his head—I can't. It's impossible to bridge the gap.

"But you did it before. Return to me! Please, come back to me, Michaels!"

—You don't understand, Mandy. I only came to deliver the letter.

Ah, she thought, *Jake's yellowed letter written when we were kids. Jake's letter had a PS that read: I promise I'll come back. Somehow, some way, I shall contact you.*

—I became conscious before the building collapsed, and Jake spoke about you. Your brother died because of me, and I made a promise to give you his wallet with the letter and the key to his apartment. I was allowed one trip back to fulfill that promise. I've stayed too long.

"No. I won't accept that you have to go back!"

Don't cry, he mouthed. Please don't cry. I can't bear it.

A blinding light flashed where Michaels was standing.

Miranda blinked her eyes, and whoosh, he was gone.

So was the dog, Ashes.

The ruins of the WTC spun, and she swayed on her feet. "Michaels, come back," she cried.

Ashes from the WTC swirled around her ankles—ashes smelling like Old Spice Cologne. The ashes caressed her, rising from the ground and whirling around her. Hot breath stirred wisps of her hair.

Mandy, a beloved voice whispered in her ear.

She spun her head around.

There was no one behind her.

Yet, she felt his arms around her and his lips at her ear.

My Mandy.

An invisible hand cupped her cheek.

She laid her hand on top of his. "I can feel you. Stay with me, Michaels," she cried.

And if this shall be my last breath, I will love you even more after death, he whispered.

She reached out blindly but no one was there.

Still, she felt his presence.

A light touch rubbed against her lips like the wisp of a feather.

There was the faintest stirring beside her.

His spirit was getting weaker. She was losing him.

"Michaels, don't go! I love you!"

There was a gust of frigid wind followed by an unearthly silence—New York City had finally shut up.

§

Chapter 50:1

And if this shall be my last breath,
I will love you even more after death.

In the stillness, Miranda could see the Twin Towers rise from the ashes of Ground Zero until the towers stood as they once were in all their glory, dwarfing the skyscrapers around them.

The Towers bustled with people and activity. Revolving doors opened. Men and women checked their watches, hurrying in to work to start their day. Elevators rose to top floors. Some employees sat at their desks eating breakfast, while others spoke on the phone with customers. Some men and women laughed with co-workers at the coffee pot while others read e-mail. They all settled in for a day like any other work day.

Then bam!

Miranda jumped and looked over to where the noise had come from.

Workmen excavated, trying to recover...*my heart.*

Once again she could see the Twin Towers rise from the ashes like matching tombstones.

How many futures did this tragedy destroy?

Jake—*he worked at a startup for a dream that would never be.*

Michaels—that this should happen to me now is one of the great ironies, he had said.

Her own—My Love, I have to go. I'll meet you later here at Ground Zero. I'll wait for you as long as it takes. Forever, if need be, I'll wait, Michaels had said.

And so, Miranda stood at the ruins of the World Trade Center.

And she waited.

Someday we'll be together again.
Just you and me.
Just you and me.
And I will always love you.

§

Epilogue

Next Train for Paradise.
All aboard!

There is a world where time stands still. The Twin Towers fade in and out, appearing like ghosts. At the entrance to the WTC Subway Station fog swirls about the subway railing, engulfing the stairs leading down to the subway terminal.

Down.

Down to the dimly lit subway station, looking like when it was first built, before graffiti writers scribbled on the walls. The station even smells like a newborn babe, of talcum powder, lotion and shampoo.

There is only one train. Train Zero. Line Z. The red line. The line leading to infinity. One way. No going back.

And so they gather at the subway stop, the ghosts of 9/11.

Some hold briefcases.

Others read newspapers.

Some sip from cups of coffee, cups that never empty. The coffee is always hot.

Some wear police uniforms or business suits. Others dress in skirts or as waiters. Some proudly wear the uniform of a fireman or dress casually as tourists. A few wear the uniform of a janitor. Their faces are the colors of the United Nations.

Like Miranda, the ghosts of 9/11 wait patiently.

They wait for the blinding headlights of the WTC Subway train to take them to their final destination.

And sitting on a bench, munching a donut, sits Jake with Ashes, the little dog who went to work with him every day, napping under his desk, the Shih Tzu whose real name was Milhouse.

Jake stands and stretches, flexing his angel's wings.

Milhouse bounces on his paws beside Jake, his own little wings fluttering in the breeze.

§

Eulogy to 9/11

And so it is finished.

Do not weep on my account.
For I have been freed from
The confines of this life
And of this body.
My spirit soars above the trappings
Of wealth.
Ambition.
Greed.
Where I am there is no need.
I am there.
Yet I am here.
Do not forget that I am with you always.
Beside you.
Inside you.
I still am conscious.
I am still me.
The essence of my being
Has not changed.
Merely the physical.
I went to sleep.
And I have awoken.
Transformed.
My memory is intact.
My heart is still full.
My personality was always my essence.
Some call it my soul.
It is indestructible.

Like my love for you.
I will not forget you.
No matter how long I must wait.
And in the meantime
Think of me.
Not with sadness.
But with joy.
For the time we had together.
And the eternity yet ahead of us.
And if this shall be my last breath,
I will love you even more after death.

Belinda Vasquez Garcia

I Will Always Love You Video - http://magicprose.com/9-11/

Other Links

Other Books by Belinda Vasquez Garcia:
http://astore.amazon.com/thewitcnarr-20

Facebook Fan Page - http://www.facebook.com/AuthorBelinda

Blog - http://belindavasquezgarcia.com/blog/

Website - http://belindavasquezgarcia.com

Twitter - http://www.twitter.com/MagicProse
(Belinda V. Garcia@MagicProse)

YouTube channel - *Belinda V Garcia.*

An Afterword by the Author

Like everyone else in the country and around the world, I felt such shock when the events of 9/11 unfolded. I had traveled to the City often to see family, and fell in love with New York on my very first visit. Writing this love story was a way for me to deal with the emotion that 9/11 left me with. The first draft was started four months after September 11, 2001, but I withheld publishing. Then and now, *I Will Always Love You* is my valentine to New York City.

To me, 9/11 was an event of Biblical proportions, especially given the religious fanaticism driving the terrorists to blind hatred. We had been spared war on our land since the attack on Pearl Harbor. We just entered the Millennium and a brave new world. I chose, therefore, to include, before each chapter a snippet of Biblical-inspired verse relating to 9/11, in what I call *New Revelations, Year I of the Millennium.*

I thank you from the bottom of my heart for buying *I Will Always Love You.*

About the Author

Belinda Vasquez Garcia is an award-winning, best-selling, critically acclaimed author. She is a native of California. Before writing full time, she worked as a Software Engineer and Web Developer. She holds a Bachelor's degree in Applied Mathematics. She lives with her husband Bob, dog Toby, and cat Shakespeare.

Return of the Bones, Inspired by a True Story, won 2014 International Latino Book Awards for BEST HISTORICAL FICTION, BEST AUDIO BOOK, and BEST EBOOK. It was the winer of the 2013 New Mexico / Arizona Book Awards for BEST HISTORICAL FICTION.

Her first book in the *Land of Enchantment Trilogy*, *The Witch Narratives Reincarnation* (Book 1), is a First Place winner of a 2013 Latino BOOKS INTO MOVIES AWARD and won a 2013 International Latino Book Award for BEST FANTASY.

Ghosts of The Black Rose (Book 2) won a 2014 International Latino Book Award for BEST FANTASY.

To keep up with Belinda's books, like her Facebook fan page: *https://www.facebook.com/AuthorBelinda*

Author Website
http://belindavasquezgarcia.com

15166078R00148

Made in the USA
San Bernardino, CA
17 September 2014